ROGUE EVENT

J. M. Erickson

Rogue Event

Copyright 2015 J. M. Erickson
Revised: January 10, 2016
http://www.jmericksonindiewriter.com

Editors: *Kirkus Editing* and Suzanne M. Owen
Cover design: Cathy Helms, *Avalon Graphics, LLC*
http://www.avalongraphics.org/

Publisher: J. M. Erickson
http://www.jmericksonindiewriter.net

ISBN: (Paperback) 978-1-942708-09-4
ISBN: (MOBI Format) 978-1-942708-19-3
ISBN: (ePub Format) 978-1-942708-20-9

This is a work of pure fiction. While some places in this book exist, any resemblance to real people, living or dead, or events is purely coincidental.

Printed in the United States of America

Other Works by J. M. Erickson

Action/Adventure Thrillers

Albatross: Birds of Flight—Book One (Revised)
Raven: Birds of Flight—Book Two
Eagle: Birds of Flight—Book Three
Falcon: Birds of Flight—Book Four
Flight of the Black Swan

Action/Adventure Science Fiction

Future Prometheus I: Emergence & Evolution—Novellas I & II
Future Prometheus II: Revolution, Successions & Resurrections—Novellas III, IV & V
Intelligent Design: Revelations
The Prince: Lucifer's Origins
Intelligent Design: Apocalypse
Intelligent Design: Revelations to Apocalypse
Future Prometheus: The Series

Book Reviews

"Some of the writing was downright lyrical in the simple elegance of the prose, and other times I was nearly breathless from the intensity and violent passion." - **Stacy Decker,** *Indie Book Reviewers*

"I was chilled by the world the author envisions and saddened by the concept of a corporate state that has hints of the world Orwell feared and overtones of Patrick McGoohan's pioneering series from the 1960s, *The Prisoner.*" - **Jack Magnus,** *Readers' Favorite*

"It is both descriptive and has *great* world building (important for a fantasy-sci/fi) but also is fast moving and unpredictable so that you aren't bored." - **Karen Matthews,** *Indie Book Reviewers*

"…a dystopian concept that fits nicely alongside the stories of Huxley and Orwell." – *US Review of Books*

"Even though there are some familiar "Orwellian" elements present, Erickson gives a fresh perspective that works so well in the context of this story." - **Cody Brighton,** *Indie Book Reviewers*

"*Rogue Event* is an engaging science fiction novel that paints a chilling picture of life in the 22nd century. Imagine our world where people are encouraged to be devoid of emotions and are brainwashed to be efficient and productive so that most of them behave like robots." - **Maria Beltran,** *Readers' Favorite*

Setting

A Different World

A century from now, Earth is united into one global organization under the governing body called Central Corporate Command & Mainframe Control. People on the surface are primarily urban dwellers in great cities focused on various business operations that keep the world economy going. The surface citizens are organized in ranks based on their levels of productivity, expertise, and efficiency. These attributes are valued while other attributes, such as emotions, are seen as disruptive and distracting.

Other sectors outside the urban settings are the agricultural industry, the ocean farming industry, and power production. Production of geothermal and nuclear energy is done in human-constructed, underground city–size caverns. There are nine located around the world.

The lunar colony in Peary Crater remains a science center that looks beyond the surface cities' narrow focus of business and economy. In 2071 the lunar colony declared its independence, having consolidated renewable energy sources, discovered water, and possessing a self-contained food chain already established for decades.

The alliance between the moon and surface cities is cooperative but distant. All scientific discoveries are filtered through the cities' governing body, Central Corporate Command. All other information in forms predating 2030—books, artwork, plays, performing arts—are heavily regulated and excluded, as it would detract from productivity and efficiency. All relevant information and data are assessed and relayed to all global surface citizens via the Mainframe Control. All other human sectors—agriculture, ocean farming, and power plant production—are allowed to receive global urban broadcasts. All sectors do so with the sole exception of the underground power plants. They prefer minimal contact.

Just over a century ago, a large rogue planet was discovered heading toward the outer edge of the Sol System. With no chance of collision, initial fears subsided and Earth's business went on. The rogue planet is now just years away from passing harmlessly by the Earth...rather, it is expected to pass harmlessly by...

Eden—Part One

Earth—AD 2134—Ruins of Merrimack College, Twenty-five Miles from Boston, Massachusetts

The rose grows among thorns. —The Talmud

"Dad! We're not supposed to be here! Mom will be angry!" Marsha said

"We're not going to tell her, Marsha," Gabriel Lawless said. He looked back at his seven-year-old daughter and smiled at her level of concern and worry. In front of him, his nine-year-old son Marvin was helping him pull weeds and collapsed wood from a recess that led to a basement. He was far more adventurous than his younger sister. Years of undergrowth, dense brush, and barriers of trees made finding the ruins difficult. If it weren't for an ancient map of the old suburbs, he was positive he never would have found it. And like so many other former suburbs of the early twenty-first century, this gold mine of history had been retaken by nature as the capital cities grew toward the sky and people were placed in their housing by the corporation.

It must have been something to pick your own place. To live where you wanted. Wow!

Gabriel pulled himself from his thoughts and looked at his son pulling more underbrush out and sweating up a storm.

Surprisingly, he found the lack of constant drones, rail vehicles and aircraft noise unnerving. The sounds of nature with its rustling trees, birds and insects were strange to his urban senses.

"You'll both be going to private school next year and this might be the last of our adventures for a long time," he said. Gabriel became sad at the thought of his children heading off to school to be inducted into the rigorous, corporate training ground of Central Corporate Command & Mainframe Control Training Camp for the Northeast Sector.

Why do they call it a "camp"? A camp is where you go to swim and hike, not to learn about compound average growth and medical health actuarial computations.

"Dad? Do you think it's another sealed-up library like the other place we found?" Marvin asked.

"I don't think so, son. This looks like this leads to a basement of an old educational building. Maybe they have books there, but it's probably something else." Gabriel returned to helping his son as his daughter took on the role of lookout. Now used to the heat, bugs, and sounds of wildlife, the trio had little fear of encountering anyone in the "old sectors." With the rise of corporations decades ago and the fall of national governments, citizens' roles were clearly outlined—those who could not handle the rules of corporate society would be relegated to either farming in the agrarian or ocean sectors or to working two miles underground in one of the power plants within the Earth's crust. Once in a great while, there were more "brilliant" deviants who were sent to the lunar colonies, but that had stopped when the colonists discovered water and a near infinite source of solar power collectors and renewable energy and material and declared their independence decades ago.

What balls, he thought

"How we doing, Marsha?" Gabriel asked in jest. As serious as a sentry protecting country, flag, and home, she responded with all earnestness.

"All clear."

Gabriel hid his smile and needed to pull hard to get through more brush and debris. His shirt and pants were now soaked with sweat, but the bug bites no longer bothered him. He was personally thrilled to be out of his hideous gray corporate suit and thus "out of uniform" to explore this hidden gem just outside the Boston metropolis.

"Figures we'd find this on the longest day of the year," Gabriel said.

"What does that mean?" his son asked.

"Longest day of the year is when our part of the world is exposed to the most light. More than fourteen hours or so of daylight. Makes for a very hot day. And the work we're doing is making us sweat pretty badly," he said.

Marvin nodded and continued.

Gabriel stood up and stretched his aching back. He wiped his brow and took a moment to go through his sweaty pants pockets. He found a small notebook with elastic bands holding down some pages for easy access. He tried to dry his hands of perspiration to keep the paper from getting wet. He found the page with the set of numbers: 42.6677° N, 71.1225° W.

"What are those numbers, Dad?" Marsha asked.

Gabriel smiled at his daughter's curiosity, a rare attribute frowned upon by Central Corporate Command.

"Longitude and latitude. They are the geographic location of this place. Think of it as a primitive GPS system. Before those, we had maps, and these were the numbers that told us where we were and where we wanted to go," he explained.

"That is really smart," Marsha said.

Gabriel nodded and saw that Marvin looked as if he were getting close to some door or hatch.

After five more minutes of excavation, Gabriel and his two children stood in front of a locked metal door. Gabriel looked at the three large locking devices that were far more recent than the door itself. He took his time to look all around the door and then expanded his search to include vicinity. He was happy he'd explained to the kids what he was looking for because it was Marsha that found letters not far from the door.

"School of Engineering," the words read. Several spaces later, more words emerged: "Fallout Shelter."

"Wow! Fallout shelter? This place predates 2001. Well before we found the rogue planet," Gabriel said excitedly.

Even though both children were smiling, he knew he had to explain in terms that they would understand.

"Long ago, like more than a hundred years ago when we first saw the rogue planet coming near our solar system, many people and institutions like colleges and universities built these underground bunkers to survive a massive asteroid impact. As it turns out, they put a lot of these bunkers together but never needed them. This one right here looks like it was an even older bunker that was converted into a kind of an ark. You see? The door is far older than the locks here," Gabriel pointed out.

"Why did they have these arks before we found the planet?" Marsha asked.

"Before then, I think, there might have been worries about nuclear war or civil strife," Gabriel said.

"Why would they build these things?" Marvin asked.

"Forewarned is forearmed," Gabriel said.

Gabriel noticed the silence and turned to see that his children didn't understand the ancient saying.

"'Forewarned is forearmed' means if you have warning, you can always prepare for disaster," he explained.

Both children nodded in agreement, indicating they understood. Gabriel looked back at the three large locks and was already trying to figure out how he might get through.

"Are you going to break in, Dad?" Marvin asked. There was caution even in his adventurous boy's voice.

"Well, more like 'explore' and try to see what's on the inside. Think of it as an archaeological find. And if we find that there's nothing there and it's of no use, maybe we can make it a clubhouse," Gabriel explained.

"That's great! Maybe we can hide those books we found and read!" Marsha added excitedly.

Gabriel nodded as he continued to look at the locks. He felt bad that he had to keep his reading and his exploring of the world from his wife, Rebekah. Before her promotions and rise in the corporate computer mainframe center, she might have been open to some of his interests. But she would see them now as "detracting from studies that will enhance productivity and efficiency." He could already hear these words. The distance had grown and there was little time in their marriage contract.

Gabriel pushed the negative and sad thoughts out of his head and focused on his precious moments with his children.

"You're so right, Marsha. If no one is using it, we could make it our private clubhouse. Fill it with food, drinks, and plenty of books."

"That would be so great!" Marvin said.

Earth—Part Two

AD 2137—Boston, Massachusetts

Without law, civilization perishes. —The Talmud

"Not with a bang but a whimper," Gabriel Lawless said. Hands resting face down on the kitchen table, he blocked out the small galley's three news monitors. The constant flow of data, news, and important stories was continuously assaulting his senses. While he and his wife were lucky to have an eat-in kitchen, his time in their home, one of thirty units outside Boston proper, was up. He looked at the third page of the glowing tablet that requested his signature. He had been on that page for twenty minutes. He looked up to see that another assessment of the incoming rogue planet that was to brush the solar system was running. It was years away but the story was running constantly.

While Marvin and Marsha were already at school, he was left alone in his kitchen with the news in the background and his wife talking into her earpiece. He could hear her getting dressed and moving around as she spoke. Her voice was strong yet feminine, a quality he had loved about her fifteen years ago. Her dark hair and matching eyes were still her best features. But their twelve-year marriage contract was up and she did not want to sign up for another twelve years.

Gabriel sniffled. The change in temperature from summer to fall was still difficult, even though most of the planet's allergens had been eliminated. He was sure it wasn't allergies. He looked up at the neat, color-coded stacks of medication to stabilize each family member's mood, lessen anxiety, and help each person focus. For the longest time, his wife's bottle had seemed always in need of refilling. After just a year, it was his wife's and both children's medication that were regularly prescribed, ordered, and taken religiously. His bottle remained untouched.

Maybe if you took your pills, this whole thing could have been avoided.

He stared back at the page and thought about walking away without signing it, but then his visitation rights, four quarterly supervised eight-hour visits, would be annulled as well. He broke his gaze and looked back up only to see that one of the three monitors was updating the world about the rogue planet hurtling just outside their solar system. After nearly a century of observation, it was only three years away from passing by at unfathomable speed. With little fear of the planet having any ramifications for the Earth and moon bases, he looked back down at where he was supposed to sign.

"Gabriel? Are you all right?" his soon-to-be ex-wife said. She was readjusting a decorative earpiece to maintain her communication link with her work. She made further minor adjustments in her attire, a black suit with a crisp white blouse. All her accessories were gold and her shoes were perfectly matched. He took his time answering her. After all the arguments, mostly one-sided, there was really nothing more to say. *All right? No, I'm not all right. How can you turn off love? How can you people do it?*

His gray suit was wrinkled and unkempt. He had sat at the kitchen table all night.

"I'm just reading some of the specifics," he answered. He looked back down and pretended to read. In an unusual gesture of kindness, she walked toward him and stood above him. She finally spoke in a tone that closely resembled compassion rather than her usual logic-driven verbiage.

"I know you love the children, Gabriel, but you have not been able to make the treatments work and you continue to be less productive," she said.

"I can try again, Rebekah," he said.

"Your lack of supervising Marvin's and Marsha's medication regimen was an act of commission rather than omission. It affected their schoolwork and productivity."

"But they don't need it…"

"You can make that decision for yourself. This lack of compliance with medical guidelines for our children is a violation of trust and what we agreed to," she said coolly.

Gabriel bit the inside of his mouth and stared back down at the third page. Without missing a beat, she continued.

"Gabriel, this obsession with remaining free of reason and subjecting yourself to emotions is harmful in the long run. You cannot manage them, and it will affect our children. Do you really want that? Do you really want to encourage their emotions and hinder their reason and growth?" she asked. Her concern was palpable.

"I can change," Gabriel started. "I can reduce my time at home and increase my time at work. Become more productive—"

"Will you start taking your medication and go into cognitive rehabilitation again?"

Gabriel remained quiet. He couldn't find the words to respond.

"I see. Well, then, that is your answer. You come from an

old school of thought that believes that children should play and embrace emotions. Even when you have shortened your time with them, you have encouraged fanciful thinking, strong emotions, and even play," she countered.

"I know, Rebekah. I'm sorry."

"We are beyond that now. I know you want Marvin and Marsha to fit in, to be productive. You can't help yourself."

"I wasn't always like this. I can change, go back..." Gabriel felt his desperation leveling, but another emotion was moving in.

"You changed when you became a father. The doctors say it happens to people sometimes. Men rarely. But your uncontrollable drive to spend time exploring their inner worlds and imaginations is intolerable. You are encouraging them to embrace things that are erratic, unpredictable, and chaotic. Those books, those novels you read to them were just another manifestation of the disease, Gabriel. You can't change something if you don't think it's a problem." The transition from compassionate to clinical was seamless.

Anger. The feeling is anger.

Gabriel didn't look up. He remained motionless for a moment until he raised his left hand and signed the document. He closed the document and handed her the tablet with his right hand. As he stood up, he felt his skin sticking to his own clothes. He moved to put his long gray overcoat on over his gray suit with gray shirt and tie and collect his meager bags to take with him.

"How long have you been ambidextrous?" Rebekah asked. Her clinical tone was not laced with anger.

Damn.

He didn't look up at her and tried to move a little quicker to get out of the kitchen, which was getting smaller by the second. He felt more anger swelling in his heart and his chest. His attempts were halted as she put her body between him and the doorway.

"This is the ninth time I have seen you use your left hand with precise fine-motor control as if you were natural at it. There have been twelve other times over the course of the last three years that I saw you change from left to right quickly in the hopes of not being detected. Are you ambidextrous? Is this yet another secret?" Rebekah asked.

Gabriel stood in front of her. Even though they were the same height, her demeanor and posture made her look taller.

"I don't know what you're talking about. May I pass, Rebekah? I need to go to work. Be productive," he said. The words sounded right but he could hear the venom in each syllable.

"Your habit of reading unauthorized, non-instructional material has led to your undoing, Gabriel. Is there more you should tell me so I can help?" she said.

Gabriel looked at her, right into her dark brown eyes. All the years of keeping his fiction reading secret, his own writing hidden and at times destroyed, things he created with his mind all kept from the woman he thought might wish to share in them. Even something as simple as being both left- and right-handed was something not well received by the majority. It was efficient to be either right-handed or left-handed but not *both*. All his neighbors and coworkers struggled with him and the free range of emotions he buried. And now he was not well received by the figment of the former wife he had long ago imagined to be a kindred spirit. The sad thought added quickly to his swelling anger. It surfaced in a burst of sweat on his brow and heat all over his body.

"Does it matter now, Rebekah? I am nothing to you and a

ghost to my children. I know you've already found another prospective mate. I'm sure he will be a proper, productive stepfather who will be the litmus test of correctness. I am sure you will speak of him as the foil of me and he will be the one that demonstrates the right way to act, while I will be seen as a social failure and unproductive citizen destined to work the factory mines out west or on the moon."

"This is what I mean, Gabriel. This emotional response to a simple question is unnecessary," she said. She put her hands up to stop his tirade but it pushed him further. Still gripping his luggage, he felt his back straighten and his movements slowly gravitate toward her. The next words were measured and were more likely unexpected.

"Rebekah, do you want to really see what 'emotional response' I can give you?" he said. With each word he had taken a step closer to her. The desired result was finally achieved. It was as if an old memory of being a mammal, fear, finally awoke out of its slumber and she realized she was in danger. Never before having experienced rage and such violent thoughts toward Rebekah, Gabriel watched his now former wife move quickly out of his path. His use of intimidation toward her was both satisfying and upsetting. He had never been menacing before. But it made him feel as if he were in control of something. Finally.

He continued from the kitchen into the small hallway that led to the door. By the time he was outside, the sweat on his head and entire body was no longer cold and clammy. Without looking back, he followed the momentum of the throngs of workers in their black, blue, brown, and even a few gray suits heading to work. The high-pitched sounds of low-flying law enforcement surveillance drones competed with the constant flow of rail traffic and heavy aircraft forever circling the metropolis. For the first time in a long time, the perpetual city noises bothered him. He thought back to when he and the kids found the old fallout shelter outside the city limits. He felt his chest tighten as he walked and tears form in the corners of his eyes. As one of millions walking to work or taking public transportation, his thoughts drifted to both his children's pictures and the novels he had in his bag.

If they find these books I'll be screwed, he thought.

The gray skyline of the city towered over everything, leaving just the illumination of the streetlamps and monitors to show the way in the early morning darkness. He passed another set of street monitors, a pair of which were displaying news and local updates while another pair monitored the area. He had a sudden fear that maybe the city's collaboration with local business had implemented the X-ray/facial recognition surveillance cameras. He felt more sweat on his forehead and looked down as he walked. He pushed the thought out of his head. As if to make matters worse, he remembered one of the books he had found years ago in an old building set to be destroyed. He struggled to remember the name of the small book. It was a year, he remembered. The author's name came to him in a flash. George Orwell.

AD 2138—Boston, Massachusetts

Every man will surely have his hour. —The Talmud

Gabriel looked out at the gray, white, and dark city skyline. Even with an unusually bright sun and few clouds, his heart was heavy and dark. Somehow the sun seemed cooler and distant. He was one of the very few who would take a break from his work to take in the vista to clear his mind and think happier thoughts. Even with the drone and aircraft noise, it was still a break. He was not feeling it though.

Not today.

Passably dressed in his usual gray suit, he clutched a folded picture of his two children, now a year older. It was deep in the pocket of his pants which were held up by an ill-fitting belt that needed more holes to be useful. His memory fluttered back to when he'd filled out his suit and all his clothes. He was swimming in them now, as his memories darkened to months gone by.

At his first visit with his children following his marital discharge, he'd felt a chasm, a gulf between himself and his beloved children. After only three months, they were focused on dates, facts, and current events. Even with prodding, they seemed no longer interested in the past, stories, creative ideas, or even dreams. The medication, extra courses, and tutors had seized them. On his third visit, only his daughter arrived. His son had sent him a brief typed note indicating that the time allotted together was inefficient, and that he could better use the time for his studies. His daughter came because she wanted to show him all of her grades and high marks on calculus, chemistry, and linguistics. She, too, needed to limit her time. She needed to be "more efficient."

Now, with his hands deep in his pockets, he pulled out a color photo of both his children. Even as he unfolded it, he still hoped that somehow the picture might magically change. Such a wish was indicative of "personal barriers," but he still wished for the magic to happen. It did not. Both children were dressed in functional school uniforms, the color image capturing the rich darks and lights of their dark clothes and stark surroundings. Their youthful looks were nearly gone and their eyes were sharp and clear but devoid of light. He stared at the recently printed picture and looked again at the time stamp of the image. It was the date and time they were supposed to meet for their scheduled quarterly visit two days ago. No apology or excuse. Just a quick message: *Over-scheduled. Will be more efficient and will make next scheduled session.*

He had no idea who wrote it. It could have been one of them or their mother. He looked back up at the sky to find the sun was now blocked by darker clouds.

"It doesn't matter," he said.

He opened his slender fingers and let the piece of paper with his children's images flutter in the wind. It was a gentle breeze. At forty-five stories high, he had expected more of a canyon effect and stronger winds.

It always was strong. He watched the paper slip over the building's edge. He paused for just a moment at the thought of following it down. He was close to the edge, and with no railing, three short feet would bring him over.

They really should have a protective rail. But then, why would you do that? Suicide is an anomaly. No need to put a rail up. It would be inefficient.

He moved closer to the edge at first and stopped before he completed even his next step closer.

"No!" a woman's voice yelled.

Gabriel turned quickly, startled by the voice and the urgency. He caught himself and saw a familiar woman he often passed in the elevator. She was one of thousands that worked in the actuaries department. But she stood out. What singled her out was that she, too, was in the minority, also wearing a gray suit but looking more disheveled. It was also surprising that she was on the roof at all. It was unusual to have anyone take a break from their screen. With all the interactive communication and gaming available, a break at the workstation was preferred by most.

"Were you going to jump?" she said. Her tone and voice were racked with emotions.

"No. I was just thinking," Gabriel said. He tried to calm his voice and be less emotional. Then he remembered that it was the woman who'd actually cried out.

"Are you all right? You sound, ah, distressed?" he asked. Suddenly Gabriel felt the corners of his mouth curl ever so slightly. He watched the woman quickly compose herself and look down as if she were checking her light gray suit for lint.

"I have heard reports of people actually committing suicide as a result of the approaching rogue planet," she said matter-of-factly. Her tone and report would have been more believable if she weren't flushed and if she hadn't displayed such deep emotions earlier. Gabriel had not seen such embarrassment in years. Maybe once when he was dating Rebekah and a few times when Marsha was younger. He stood quietly and embraced the moment. He had forgotten what she had said and realized he was staring.

"I'm sorry. Suicide?"

"Yes. There were two suicides three months ago," she said. She was now looking up at him. The expression was actually readable. Her look of surprise at his not knowing about the suicides was obvious.

"I'm sorry. I am not as productive and efficient as my coworkers. I tend to turn off my monitors in my residence. It quiets my mind," he said. Again he was pleasantly surprised at her display of emotions.

"Well, um, all right. There was a couple who jumped off the Leverett Data Collection Building. They left a note that they wanted to end their lives before we all died," she explained.

Unfamiliar with the specifics, Gabriel was aware that there had been some initial panic when a rogue planet bigger than Jupiter was first spotted heading well outside the solar system. But that was a century ago when emotions ran high.

When did we lose them? Was it when the corporations took over?

Gabriel shook his head as if to help clear his thoughts and remembered what the woman had just said so he could respond.

"But that doesn't make sense. The science community and all the experts say it will pass like a comet," he said. After nearly ten decades of seeing the rogue planet approaching, the data and research, computer models and extrapolations were clear that its passing would be remarkable but far from dangerous. Secretly, though, he wondered if it was all lies.

They would keep it secret, those bastards! Focus, Lawless...focus.

"Yes. Quite true," she said. She turned suddenly and began to walk quickly away. Gabriel felt a sudden urge to call out, which he promptly did.

"Oh, I'm sorry. What's your name?" He stepped forward to try to narrow the gap. She turned quickly to look at him.

"My name is Veronica," she said. She turned swiftly again and was nearly running to the roof door. Gabriel watched her leave and felt both curious and sad. He was sad that she was gone. With her name, finding her would be easy. Still, he held on to the brief moment of raw emotions he had experienced both alone and with another human. It was confusing and wonderful at the same time. For the first time in a year, the odd yet unique interaction had made him happy.

AD 2139–Boston, Massachusetts

Who can protest and does not is an accomplice in the act. —
The Talmud

Gabriel walked slowly by Veronica's work area next to the elevators. It was still empty. With all of his work collected for the ride to his small efficiency residence, he wondered where she had been all afternoon. He had left her a treasured artifact. After several months of a silent exchange of novels and poetry, he pushed aside the thought that she might have betrayed him. He forced himself to look away and stand with his back against the working space facing the elevator. Much to his chagrin, the elevator came nearly immediately. He stepped on and moved to the back, prolonging the stay until he finally turned around and saw that her work area was still empty. The elevator was silent except for breathing, as everyone was watching something on their eyeglass computer wear.

I wonder where she is.

More stops came and went with more silent people getting on the elevator.

I wonder what it must have been like when music used to play in elevators.

With the car filled to capacity, Gabriel looked blankly at the back of mostly women's heads. Devoid of glasses with personal settings, he looked straight ahead rather than look at the four monitors by the floor readers. He had already got his dose of news. In addition to not wearing his personal eyewear, he had the only gray suit in the elevator. There were fewer and fewer of them at his level as they would either be reassigned or promoted. While his suit could have fit him just a tiny bit better, he was not inclined to get a new one.

I'm never going to get a new suit, he thought. It was a defiant thought. One of many he'd harbored throughout the day, every day for the last two years. Still, he looked blankly ahead amid the silence of humanity engrossed in their personal entertainment. In his head, he turned over the last message he'd received from Rebekah, about terminating his parental rights. After a full year of no contact with his children, and with his ex-wife looking to "union" with another man who was "significantly more productive and efficient," Gabriel had declined to sign the document even under threat of a competency hearing.

I hope Veronica is all right.

Finally the elevator doors opened to the large building foyer with its perfectly pruned and predictable trees, floors, and grass arranged around a decorative waterway. In the midst of moving suits in black, brown, and various shades of dark blue, rows of flowers lay in neatly arranged beds surrounded by running water and still, small pools. The only thing that spoiled the natural scene were various delivery drones flying like large birds above his head. Still, he would always look at the flowers and look for the changes that were made every third Tuesday. He walked carefully to fit in like so many workers with their computer wear and tablets. In addition to having a gray suit, he was nearly the only one with a briefcase. A portfolio, really. He was sure they all thought he had a laptop and other "manual" material. He calmed himself at the very thought of his novella in the recessed pocket with all of his personal writing. He suppressed a smile at the thought of writing his own story.

Colonel Walter Kurtz, he thought. *What would you think of this heart of darkness?*

He looked up to see the water again and wondered who arranged and did the work. It hinted to some degree of creativity, and it looked pretty. Two concepts that went against the well-established norms of consistency, productivity, and efficiency.

Marring the constructed natural sight were several banks of monitors with ongoing news that spilled over the flowers. While there was no sound but instead closed-captioning, the water could still be heard over the din of shoes and high heels clicking away. The lack of human voices talking no longer surprised him. He looked at a larger monitor and was struck by the vision of a large celestial body, a large planet, gracefully floating by. He slowed to a stop and approached the monitor. He was surprised by how clear and real-looking the image was before him. He was puzzled. To date, Central Corporate Command & Mainframe Control had always provided detailed animation and representation rather than actual satellite pictures. The decision to send satellites to meet and explore the rogue planet had been dismissed decades ago as a monumental waste of taxes, time, and productivity.

He stood and read the captions. He must have looked like a child staring at a new toy. He suddenly wondered if toys were still made. Finally, Gabriel saw why the satellite pictures looked real. They were, in fact, real transmissions. He did his best to suppress a smile and to look as disinterested as possible. He pulled his hand away from stroking the stubble on his chin. The unconscious behavior had already drawn the attention of his supervisor. "Not appropriate," she had stated in her disciplinary memorandum.

He looked closely at the massive size of the dark planet as closed captions scrolled by. After all the reports of how the lunar colonies had wasted resources, time, and money to simply witness and explore the event, new data about the rogue planet's actual trajectory, speed, and composition had come to light. The next images were of celebrating humans on the moon in their multicolored, different style clothing and a disarray of material all around their command and control center. The people looked pale, larger, but enthusiastically happy.

Were they always this emotional? Happy? Were all of them celebrating?

The image then shifted to more lunar citizens in larger areas all rejoicing wildly by Earth standards with public displays of affection such as kissing. But just as suddenly, many of the more official members looked surprised and gravely concerned. And that is when the live transmission ended and more information on power consumption came online.

Wow.

Gabriel pulled himself away from the monitors for fear that he would break down in joy, grief, or both. He was thrilled to see that such liberal expression of emotions was possible. But then *those* people were all on the moon or two miles under the Earth's crust. He tried to pick up his pace to get out of the building in case his actions had been noticed by either security or human resources. He clutched his portfolio as he moved quickly.

I was born at the wrong time, wrong place.

21

He walked straight to the building's doors with his head held down to avoid eye contact. Not that it mattered, with everyone watching their own programming on their computer wear. He had often fantasized about requesting to go to the moon or work in the Earth's crust. While getting to the moon would be a problem now that it was independent and its own sovereign world, becoming a "miner" in the underground nuclear power and thermal heating power plants would be far easier.

All you have to do is cry. Laugh. Be happy...be human...I wonder why they all got serious all of sudden.

A sudden surge of anger began to form in the pit of his stomach. He pushed the glass door with more force than he'd expected. He could feel the looks he was getting from those closest to him. In the sea of black, brown, and blue suits, he felt self-conscious. He would have continued in his dark thoughts except he saw a woman he knew. Slowing his pace, he quickly evaluated the situation. Surrounded by the building's security team and the human resources director, the petite woman in the gray suit looked ashen and tearful.

Veronica? What?

He slowed down more to listen in to what the emotionless human resources officer was saying.

"It is clear that you watched the rogue planet images and teared up. When I attempted to see you, you left the building," the officer said.

"It is time to go home," she said weakly.

"You are second shift, Ms. Sykes. You are not designated to leave your work area. Further, you demonstrated more emotional leakages this past week and avoided your sessions with Dr. Breitbart for treatment," the man continued.

"I-I forgot," Veronica started.

"Negative," a female officer said. "You were reminded one hour before today. When I came to find you, you had left your work area again. What is in your portfolio?"

Gabriel clutched his own bag. Then he realized that the security officer had told Veronica to open hers. His heart raced and his stomach felt like lead. Just like he and no one else, she, too, had a carrying bag.

No! She probably has my book! She's going to get into so much trouble! No!

Gabriel came to a full stop mere feet from the scene. The sea of changing shifts of dark suits continued to ebb and flow, leaving the drama to unfold. Gabriel felt a pang of sympathy. He had seen her several times over the course of the year. She would risk a short nod and even a suppressed smile whenever they would pass. Then the poetry on napkins where the other sat at break began. Beautiful poetry and then quotes. Once he reciprocated, it was as if a secret companion, a like-minded fellow, had joined him. And now she was going to be exposed.

No. I can't lose her like this, he thought.

As he stared, he saw another officer looking beyond his own computer glass wear watching the scene. Expressionless, the officer said something into his glass piece.

Compassion? Fear? Angry about hiding in the background, Gabriel felt his heart break for Veronica. Without further delay, he spoke as he approached the small group. A female officer at first moved to block his approach.

"Veronica? Are you telling on me? You're such a spy!"

Veronica's head snapped up, and looked at him. She did a poor job suppressing her surprise.

The female officer who'd first approached him came to a stop.

"What are you saying, Mr. Lawless?"

23

With little effort, he expressed himself with zeal.

What am I waiting for? I won't sign that letter! I'll never wear a suit again. I hate you all!

"What I'm saying is…is that woman has been spying on me! I can't stand it anymore!"

"Why is she spying on you, Mr. Lawless? Ms. Sykes was not enlisted to observe you nor have you reached surveillance level five," the human resources director said.

"She found my book and was going to bring it to security after I left!" he cried out.

His anger came in full force as he saw all the passersby stop to watch what must have been for them an emotional explosion in the midst of their tranquility.

I hate you all…

Gabriel pushed the female officer away and unzipped his briefcase and thrust his hand deep into the recesses to retrieve his own, worn written work and another old paperback book. Before he could even retract his hand, two sets of electrodes clipped onto his chest. Before the current from the electrodes even fired, he smiled.

"At last," he said.

A bright light flashed before him and he felt his muscles lock up and then shake as the electricity ripped through his body. He felt only his nerve endings on fire, and then the ground rushed to his face. Darkness enveloped him. Still, he felt happy.

AD 2140–En-route to Wyoming–
Two Miles under Earth's Surface

*Join the company of lions rather than assume the lead
among foxes.* —The Talmud

"So, how fast do you think we're going? Must be more than a hundred miles per hour," Gabriel said.

He didn't bother turning to hear what his companions might say. He was sure they would say nothing. Sitting in an eight-seat personal rail transport, he just couldn't contain himself. If not for the competency hearings and evaluations and finally judgment, he might have been heading in the other direction in his gray suit. He promised himself he would never wear a gray suit again. Based on his procreative competencies in producing two "productive and logical children" and a carefully constructed letter of support from his ex-wife, the court was willing to try two years of readjustment treatment and immersion therapy. But it didn't work out that way.

Instead, Gabriel Lawless was wearing a bright orange jumpsuit in shackles looking out of a speeding dark tunnel as he was whisked along to Deep Station Power Plant Six just outside of the old deserted state park once known as Yellowstone. Two point three miles deep in the planet's crust, he was on his way to join a small underground colony of miners—men and women castaways who either chose to join or were forced to join as a form of atonement, exile, and forced productivity. There were even rumors that the population had grown into a city. The station provided no reports, just power. The cities on the surface needed power, and the underground power plants around the world had provided them—nuclear and thermal for the last eighty-three years. While the nine worldwide underground stations did not declare their own independence like the lunar colonies, they behaved as such, remaining separate, silent and removed from their surface-dwelling cousins. There were even stories of the existence of dogs and cats, former pets that were eradicated on the surface due to their lack of efficiency and their tendency to inspire emotions.

Gabriel felt like an unbridled child again. Since his arrest for collecting and distributing books, especially fiction, and his lack of productivity, he had been processed as a criminal. When he awoke from his electroshock, it was as if he were a new man. As soon as he found out that Veronica had been cleared of possessing his novel—*A Tale of Two Cities*—he quietly rejoiced, and then punched his guards several times before he was subdued again. Such violent actions were not only unheard of in an ordered society, they were not tolerated. Treatments, isolation, and threats of punishment were all met with quotes, phrases, and words his captors could not understand. Still, through it all, he was always surprised to see that Dr. Samuel Breitbart, resident human specialist of Central Corporate Command & Mainframe Control for the Northeast Sector, was always there, always trying to help with his calm, soft voice, which approximated soothing better than any human or computer to date.

Seeing his own reflection in the darkness, the bright orange made Gabriel stand out from the six guards and Dr.

Breitbart. A rounded, bearded face had replaced the thin one of last year. Up four sizes, he felt light on his feet even though he had surpassed his protein quota and body mass index as a result of constant lifting of heavy things to build muscle strength. He raised his shackled hands to stroke his graying beard. He liked it and smiled. He saw Dr. Breitbart looking at him curiously in the reflection.

"So, Sam? What's the look about?"

"You are like so many I have escorted to your final destination," he said calmly.

"Am I heading to a firing squad, doc?" Gabriel had come to like the stoic, calm doctor. Throughout all the trials and hearings, Dr. Breitbart had always been trying to help save him.

A human trait, finally.

"We do not use capital punishment. It was banned seventy years ago."

"Yeah, I know that, doc. My point is I'm heading to a place that no one has ever come back from. Nothing but audio communication. Weird but it might be interesting," Gabriel said. He was apprehensive. He had requested to go to the moon, but both Earth and lunar officials had declined due to not having enough castaways to economically send to the moon at this time. If they had, the lunar government would have granted the asylum.

Instead, he was heading to the underground power plant facilities. Built more than eighty years ago as a way to protect energy sources from the ravages of weather, they started out as small groupings shortly after the lunar secession. After years of operation, all the underground cities continued generating power but went silent for the most part.

"The colonies' rationale on limiting their visual contact is to maintain social order. Their citizens know nothing of what we have. If they did, they would leave their posts. It is a unique approach. They are obviously not as free as our society," the doctor said.

Gabriel felt his eyebrows rise. He turned to look at the doctor, who seemed engrossed in something that had come across his eyeglass screens. While the other guards stood around him and watched him carefully, Gabriel laughed out loud. It startled his watchers. It took him a moment longer to collect himself before he spoke. The shift from joviality to seriousness was natural to Gabriel now, but it had to be difficult for his logical, emotionless companions.

A year of free expression will do that, he thought. With the relative quiet of the cart flying on its rails, he found himself sighing before he spoke.

"You think you're free. You are not. It is an illusion, a mirage you cling to so you can feel safe and secure. I have lived your way for thirty-nine years and watched my life slip into gray. My children vanished into the corporate and industrial system to become logical, highly productive cogs of a mindless, dead, soulless society while the woman I once loved replaced me with a substitute. I would have done anything for my family. But to be gray in a world of dark suits, and black and white? No. Two miles in the Earth's crust with no contact with *your* kind? It is better to reign in hell than to serve in heaven," Gabriel said. He looked back into the speeding darkness, sure that they had all missed his literary reference.

Milton, Dickens, Melville, Poe....I really miss my collections, he thought. That was truly his only regret.

Two hours of silence transpired until he felt the large electromagnetic personal transport decelerate to a smooth stop.

Gabriel took his time to look out the dark window and then all around the others to see if there was anything visible to see. He slowly stood up with his shackles in place and his guards moving in unison around him as he approached the door. The door hissed open and the smell of damp sulfur and heat was evident. He stepped out onto a dimly lit platform and followed Dr. Breitbart. He looked around until he finally noticed that all the guards had their computer glass wear off.

"Hey, doc, what's the deal with your electronics?"

"The tunnel's walls are at low levels of radioactivity even though they are lined with lead. No electromagnetic waves can penetrate without a direct corded line in or out."

"I guess that's another good way of keeping silent," Gabriel said more to himself than to the others.

"Yes," the doctor said. Gabriel was surprised at the level of discomfort he expressed.

"What's the matter, doc?"

Surprisingly the doctor answered quickly, as if his concerns were top of mind.

"The shielding against electromagnetic and carrier waves and all forms of wireless communications for the one route in and out of such a large complex, and the colonies' insistence on remaining isolated for years with near to no interaction with us above, has always…worried me," he said.

Gabriel looked at him a moment to consider the doctor's concern, something rarely seen in a citizen.

After a short three-minute walk down an empty metal ramp that reverberated with every step, they finally came to a large metal door. A very old case hung on the wall right beside the entrance. The doctor opened it and typed in a series of alphanumeric symbols. As soon as he retracted his hand, heavy mechanical latches and bars moved, opening the ancient door.

Gabriel watched the old door move slowly and was impressed with its thickness, which had to be close to three feet.

"Is there anything you would like to record for the transcript before you enter?" Dr. Breitbart asked. As always, it was as close an approximation to kindness as he had ever heard.

Still listening to the loud gears, Gabriel spoke as he saw the door was opening only a little bit to allow one person to squeeze by.

"'It is a far, far better thing that I do, than I have ever done; it is a far, far better rest that I go to than I have ever known.'"

Dr. Breitbart nodded as if he understood. Gabriel felt the guards move him firmly through the door's narrow entrance. Their zeal in pushing him through quickly was a testament either of their desire to unload their charge or to escape the setting or more likely both. As soon as he cleared the other side, he heard the heavy doors gears again and watched what little light there was from the outside fade. For just a moment he wondered if it was a mistake to embrace feeling and push against the system. A quick recall of the laughter, the reading, and the total expression of life over the last year flashed before him as if to confirm that it was the right choice.

Finally the door closed solidly behind him and he stood alone, shackled in darkness. After a few seconds, a female voice came over an old-fashioned intercom. A sudden hiss of air came at him from all sides and an amber light slowly emerged from the walls.

"Well, well, well, Mr. Gabriel Lawless. Quoting Charles Dickens as you depart the world above? Impressive and contextually perfect. Now what is the rest? "'It was the best of times. It was the worst of times, it was the age of wisdom, it was the age of foolishness, it was the epoch of belief, it was the epoch of incredulity…' Welcome to your final destination."

As Gabriel struggled to raise his hands to protect his face from the pelting air, he was baffled and surprised at the voice's tone and that it had registered the Dickens reference.

She knows Charles Dickens? How? Where am I? What is this all about?

Gabriel could barely talk as the voice continued. Its tone shifted from amused to instructional, as if the person had shifted personas from professor to soldier.

"Once the forced air cleans your clothes of dust and dirt, please proceed to the door at the end of the corridor. There your shackles and clothes will be removed, and you will be cleaned, processed, and welcomed to your new home."

Still in shock, Gabriel did his best to follow directions. He was surprised at how the voice had sounded pleasant, and yet it seemed to express both humor and an undertone of darkness.

Where am I?

As promised, a series of machines came to life, his shackles and clothes were removed, and he was run through a series of multiple showers of many different liquids and vapors. His skin felt just a bit raw but cleaner than he had ever experienced. At the end of all of it, he found a warm, soft red towel and a clean tan jumpsuit and comfortable shoes. Confused but free of shackles and dead skin, he was also dressed, clean and focused on the large door in front of him. He stood there quietly and waited. As with the first door, the heavy mechanical hinges stirred and the door slowly opened. While the light in the cleaning area was a low, ambient illumination, the light on the other side appeared brighter. Gabriel was afraid. Afraid of what was next, not of death. As the light grew, his mind raced to what the voice had said earlier.

"'…it was the season of Darkness, it was the spring of hope…'" he muttered.

AD 2142–Deep Station Power Plant Six, Wyoming–Two Miles under Earth's Surface

Hold no man responsible for what he says in his grief. —
The Talmud

"This is why we can't have nice things in the Welcome Center," a deep voice said.

Gabriel moaned at the voice, fully aware of who it was and where he'd most likely ended up. He forced his crusty eyes open but they were reluctant to comply. While his raging headache made itself known, his attempts to stir were rewarded with aches and pains. Lying on his side away from the voice and the seemingly bright lights, he managed to roll onto his back. Parched throat, headache settled in his forehead, and every bone in his body aching, he did his best to focus on what had happened in the last forty-eight hours.

"As always, lieutenant, Lawless lived up to his name," the deep voice said. It was without judgment but pointed out the irony of his name and the situation. Gabriel slowly moved his left hand to his left cheek. Without need of a mirror, he could tell by the swelling and the dull pain that his eye was sporting a pretty good shiner.

Just great.

"Come on, constable, this is the second time he's done this. And it's always pretty predictable; something happens on the surface and he's trying to get up there," a female voice said.

"He's been here for two years. He should know better."

"Can you blame him?"

"No, lieutenant, but we already got three new arrivals I have to watch. I don't need him giving my people combat lessons. And shouldn't he be a role model for his students? For a guy who got Teacher of the Year and who's a fiction writer, you'd think he'd be tamer," the constable complained.

"He is tame when he is focused on his students. But it's different for the newer arrivals," the female voice said.

Gabriel moaned again. He knew the voice and made the connection.

Damn it. Lieutenant Julia Rose and Chief Constable Hector Mendez. Nice job, Lawless.

"Now, you actually chose to sponsor this guy? Why do you always take on the literate dumb asses? Looking for challenges? Don't you think running the outer perimeter patrol is challenge enough?" the constable asked.

"No one's perfect, Hector," she said.

"It's a good thing his kids love him," Mendez replied.

At the mentioning of the kids, Gabriel sat up quickly. His head felt like it was going to explode, and his muscles screamed out in pain. Dizzy from his sudden movements, he leaned back against the wall for support and remained sitting in his bunk. Blurry vision finally cleared to reveal a very large pale man in a security uniform peering down at him. Beside him was a striking blonde in military uniform. Similar to the man, she, too, was pale but her form was feminine even in uniform. And while she stood a foot smaller than the constable with her hands behind her back, she exuded no less authority.

"Well, well, well…the prince returns. What is it, Mr. Lawless? 'Something is rotten in the state of Denmark?'" the lieutenant said.

It took Gabriel a few seconds to recall where the line was from. For a lieutenant in the DS6 Special Forces, Deep Station Power Plant Six's own military service, the lieutenant was both literate and had a wicked sense of humor to go along with her own brand of justice.

"You know, lieutenant, you got a line for everything. I'm guessing one of your parents was a teacher?" the constable asked.

"Both were professors. And they taught literature and history."

"The *real* history?"

"Yup. Before Central Corporate Command and the computer mainframe got rid of it all. I really do hate them," she said.

Gabriel tried to chuckle at the repartee but found it difficult to move, let alone speak or laugh. He focused on talking first. He took a moment to find the right words and syntax.

"Is it Monday…" he croaked out.

"Zero six hundred, my smelly, hungover mentee. You have at least two hours to get yourself together and get to class. And just so you know, all of your students petitioned on your behalf so you could avoid cleaning out human waste collectors. For me, I was going to have you spend a month cleaning the nature habitat in addition to human waste removal. It's a good thing you have friends, Mr. Lawless." Lieutenant Rose's voice was melodious. Very different in real life than it had seemed the first time he heard her over the intercom in the decontamination chamber for new arrivals.

"Well, at least he's not in the service. He would have been drummed out a year ago," the constable added.

"Or promoted. Once again, his efforts, however sloppy, did find a potential security breach," Rose said.

"You find a silver lining to every cloud, don't you, lieutenant?"

Gabriel carefully held his head up with one hand, and he placed another on the bunk to help push himself up. He stopped to get his wind and started again in just a moment. He smiled at the thought of his students' kindness and activism. Suddenly, he felt a pang of sadness. Sharp memories of his two children when they were much younger flooded his thoughts.

"They're still up there," Gabriel muttered.

There was an uncomfortable silence in the room. The only noise to emerge was the sliding of the transparent barrier to release him.

"I'll get you coffee to go and some aspirin," the constable said in a far more gentle voice. After two years of knowing him, Gabriel had rarely heard the officer sound compassionate.

Gabriel's field of vision was filled with Rose's image in front of him. His left eye took in less. She remained quiet, as if waiting for him to talk. At least two minutes went by before he spoke again.

"How far did I get?" he finally asked.

"You got to the Welcome Center's post screening center. It took three security officers and two civilians to take you down. I had warned them to bring stun guns but they didn't believe me that there is such a thing as 'old man strength,'" she said.

"I'm only forty-one," Gabriel said.

"And the oldest security team member who took you down was twenty-five. For all of us over thirty, we salute you."

Gabriel nodded. He moved slowly to the edge of his bunk and pushed himself up slowly to stand. It was a precarious effort with the aching in his body, head, and heart all crashing down on him at the same time.

"Gabriel…I won't pretend to know what you're going through. With only a handful of new arrivals, those of us who were born here have no idea of what it would be like to lose all that you had aboveground, again."

Gabriel caught the subtlety. The first time he lost everything was when he was arrested and started his process toward exile. That was under his control. But this time around was too much. And in a drunken state, he'd been determined to get to the surface.

What were you going to do, dumb ass? Freeze to death?

Gabriel nodded at her kindness. She extended a hand for him to move out of the stark holding cell.

"Watch your step," she pointed out.

Moving slowly, he looked around the observation room and saw that the other four cells were dark and empty. He turned to see that the plant's visual alarms were still flashing at "yellow," but they were on mute.

"Here you go, Lawless," the constable said. He had two porcelain cups of a warm, black liquid that Gabriel had learned to love. He gratefully accepted the coffee, as did the lieutenant. The constable also gave him three aspirins, which he immediately took and gulped down with some of the warm coffee. Rose thanked the security chief and continued walking through the small office into the narrow hallway.

"I want my coffee cups back, you two," the constable yelled after them. Rose waved back to him without looking and sipped her coffee as she walked.

Gabriel kept pace but did his best to savor his coffee,

walk, and not make any sudden movements unless he wanted his head to fall off. Unable to walk side by side due to the narrow space and the various security personnel, soldiers and civilians already on their way to work or home, he stayed behind her and listened. It was a very familiar pattern. She would lead and talk, and he would follow and listen.

"While you were passed out from your attempts to get to the surface, Earth Central Corporate Command & Mainframe Control finally made the announcement that the rumors that Earth escaped its orbit three days ago are true and that it was the rogue planet's unusual powerful gravity well and strong electromagnetic field that disrupted the orbit."

"Any reason why the planet's gravity well was exponentially greater than that of the sun? I mean, I'm not a science guy but it makes no sense that a planet twice as big as Jupiter could have a more powerful gravitational pull than the sun. And what did it do to our sun?"

"Tell me about it. I'm a soldier, not a scientist. They tell me, I nod as if I understand and then tell my team and they do the same," she said. She kept her pace up and sipped more of her coffee. Gabriel shook his head. It was all too big an idea to get his head around to comprehend. The lieutenant continued.

"Surprisingly, civil discord and riots were nonexistent upstairs. The surface population's overall response is to go to work late, sporadically, or not at all," the lieutenant said. The tone of surprise was easy to spot.

"Command did a real good job drugging nine billion people with pills, entertainment, and memos," Gabriel said. His anger was still hot even after two days of alcohol-induced unconsciousness.

"I know. The dimming sunlight, disrupted weather patterns, and drop in temperatures were getting hard to explain.

The surface dwellers never considered that their government might be lying," she said.

"We could have told them," Gabriel said. He didn't hide his emotion too well. Rose's response was classic.

"And then what? 'Hello, surface dwellers. Your government is lying to you, so listen up—we can accommodate five thousand of your civilians out of your nine billion people. Oh? You don't want the help? Just keep pumping the energy to us? All right…'"

It was easy to see that Rose was angry, too. For a compact woman drinking coffee, she could go from zero to one hundred herself. He sometimes forgot there were fifteen thousand other humans in their complex who might have feelings about their cousins on the surface.

"Some could have made it," Gabriel said with less anger.

"Gabriel, when we offered the Central Corporate Command places for their children, they asked us to forget them and make room for their elite and officers. When we refused, they attempted to take our complex," Rose said. It was her turn to get angry.

"I know, Rose…I was there," he said.

"Now it will take us months to cut through the debris and rebuild the transport to the surface. Maybe a year or more. And why? Because we're expendable," she said.

Even though the halls were filled with people and some dogs and cats, he felt as if he were alone with her. Finally the hall walls transitioned from solid stone to transparent aluminum and steel, granting an impressive view from above of several acres of farms illuminated with artificial lights and heated with geothermal heating. Light filled all the corridors and gave the impression of a bright, cloudless morning. It was easy to see the other connecting, transparent tubes forming a lattice of hallways all filled with people and pets.

"By then, all life will be gone on the surface, Rose," Gabriel said.

He watched Rose slow her pace to stop and look at him.

"I know, Gabriel. It's not like we didn't try to help," she said.

Gabriel looked down rather than look into her eyes, which he would always do.

"I know. It's just that it's…"

"Unfair," Rose finished. "Of course it is. A hundred years ago when we first saw this planet coming, we started the underground programs. And when Central reversed its decision, since the chance of being struck was not probable, they converted this sanctuary into power plants two miles into the Earth's crust, a great venture to power the world above. I was born here, Gabriel. My parents were born here, too, and my three children are miners like us all. It's unfair that we were relegated here. It's just crazy that we'll survive and the majority above will not."

"None of them will live…any life. Only the ones that have prepared."

The light from the farming areas subsided as the transparency changed back to natural stone. The transition to actual rock was an indication he was near the residence center.

"What's happening with the lunar colonies?" he asked. He took another gulp of his coffee. Between the movement, aspirin. and coffee, he was feeling a bit human again. Changing the subject helped.

"They're all right for now. In about five hundred years, they'll be on their own path," she said. She took another gulp of her drink.

"Oh no. Really?"

"Yup. Life imitating fiction, Mr. Lawless. Your novel last year seems prophetic. The rogue planet not only messed with our sun and the inner planets, but the moon's orbit will break from us in about five centuries. Not as sudden or dramatic as our departure but it's pretty fast in astronomical terms, I hear. They'll be on their own spacecraft. At least they have enough resources to last centuries. Who knows. Maybe this is God's way of allowing us to explore strange new worlds," Rose said with a chuckle.

"No," he said.

"That imagination of yours sure has a knack for accuracy."

Rose came to a sudden stop and turned to look right at him. She then took his empty cup and moved to retrace her steps back. Gabriel looked around and realized he was in front of the living quarters he shared with eight others.

Before continuing, she turned back to ask something.

"Hey, Gabriel? I had a chance to review the video of you battling with security..."

"Lieutenant, you have no idea how sorry I am for all of that," Gabriel started.

"No, Gabriel, I got that. I wanted to ask you about the numbers you kept yelling out," she clarified.

Gabriel squinted his eyes and furrowed his brow in the hopes that such efforts would help him remember. The whole event was a blur. It must have been obvious from his face that he was drawing a blank.

"It was something like 'forty-two, sixty-seven, zero-nine, seventy'."

The answer flooded his brain. He recited the numbers robotically as if they were engraved on his brain.

"Latitude 42.6677 and longitude 71.1225...it's a place I

used to take my kids. It was sort of a fort or clubhouse we found years ago. It was pretty deep in the ground under an old building. It was built for radioactive fallout. Maybe they remembered. I just thought, maybe..." he started.

"Maybe your children went there?" she said.

Gabriel looked down to hide the tears forming in his eyes.

"It's stupid, I know," he said.

"Hopeful, Gabriel, hopeful. Nothing wrong in being hopeful. That's what keeps us all going," the lieutenant said. She pivoted on her heels and headed back down the corridor, ostensibly to return the constable's coffee cups.

"Thank you, Rose. Sorry I've been a pain in the ass," he called back to her. She waved without even looking back. He returned the wave and then his hand went to his eye. It was hurting less, too. He was sure his students were going to give him hell for his actions.

Natural consequence for being stupid. I guess I'll be the living example of being held accountable and accepting the consequences. That's a good lesson plan for adolescents, Gabriel thought.

"Yeah, you are a pain. You got a visitor, by the way," Rose added. "She came in last week on the last transport from the surface before we blew all access to the surface. It took us some time to figure out who she was," Rose said.

Before he could ask, she was already out of view.

"The last transport from the surface? Wow. That is one lucky person. I guess he's staying with us," he mumbled.

Gabriel turned to his door, keyed in his access code, and pushed the slider open. He was only two feet into his living area when he heard a joyous cry and felt a woman jumping into his arms. Shocked by the enthusiasm and hug, he let the woman hug him tightly while she sobbed. With few options, he just rubbed her back until the weeping began to subside and her death-like grip lessened. After a few seconds, he was able to finally peel the woman away to identify who he was holding. He held her at arm's length and looked at her to make sure he was actually grasping who he thought he was holding.

"My God…it's been years…" he muttered.

He pulled her back into another hug, but it was he who squeezed and began to cry.

"Veronica…I'm so glad you're here," he said.

Purgatory—Part Three

Deep Station Power Plant Six—AD 2137—Wyoming, Two Miles under Earth's Surface

Truth is heavy, therefore few care to carry it. —The Talmud

Maria Henry was just on the verge of an orgasm when her personal communicator vibrated incessantly. She let go for as long as she could until the rising pressure and feeling of excitation melted away. The movement under the sheets slowed to a stop. Her lover of two years must have heard the vibration as well and picked up on his lost opportunity to help her release her stress. It had been a long fourteen-hour shift in the power plant's control room overseeing thousands of workers and an even larger number of citizens working to keep the underground world viable with water, artificial light, air, plants, and an entire biosphere for more than fifteen thousand people. Without even a pause, she reached over in the dimly lit room to her table and fumbled to turn on her communicator.

"It's Mark, isn't it? He has this thing about timing," her lover chuckled.

Maria found she was devoid of humor and just wanted to turn back time twenty minutes to turn off her device.

"If he wasn't so good at scheduling shifts and handling exports, I'd fire him! I was so close," she said. She pulled herself out of the bed and stood in the small room. She tapped her device and the smiling bearded icon of Mark Dempsey, energy export chief, came on. She found the annoyingly small button to turn the communicator on and end the unremitting vibrating.

"No one likes you very much, Mark! You're up too early, stay at work too long, and you're too damn clearheaded in the morning. It's my day off and I'm not even halfway through my sleeping cycle and you call me? Did we have a meltdown in Silo Eight or are the surface dwellers demanding more power?"

In a rare display of seriousness, her jovial and remarkably positive chief was far more somber than she expected. She had a fear that maybe it really was a catastrophic event.

Damage to the power plants? Biosphere?

"I'm really sorry to bother you, boss, but I got a four-person personal transport car heading to Welcome Center Three."

"That's it," she said. She felt a silk robe falling on her shoulders to cover up her naked body. She flashed a smile and worked her arms into the sleeves as she juggled the device. The robe was a gift from her paramour last year and she just loved the material. Maria was positive that Mark had caught sight of her naked breasts and her maneuvering. It wasn't the first time her chief had.

"So you get me out of bed for an unexpected transport? Maybe it's one of the gray suits, the surface walkers, calling it quits upstairs to voluntarily join us. It happens. Once, I think," she said.

Maybe twice in two decades.

"Not this time, boss. We got a call from half a mile out asking us to 'receive three packages from Lazarus.' Any idea what that means? And how the hell did they manage communication while in transport? Their electronics and communication should have all been rendered useless."

Maria froze in place. The phrase was a code she never thought she would ever hear. Maybe from some other boss thousands of years from now or later, but not now. It took her a full minute to realize that she must have looked like she'd seen a ghost.

"Okay, boss, you're scaring the shit out of me. What's the deal?" Mark asked.

His voice pulled her back. An immediate plan of action came into place. It was a well thought out protocol and operations plan. Not since the lunar bases seceded from Earth decades ago had she thought she would be pulled into a life-or-death situation on a global scale. Maria moved as she spoke.

"Mark, I want you to clear the Welcome Center of all staff and have Security Chief Mendez meet me there in ten minutes. I'll brief you later. No discussion about this, and call in Alpha shift and keep Beta shift in place. I want all data and information on this matter locked down."

"Will do, boss" was all Mark said. She ended the call and already had her pants on when she gave up looking for her bra and put her work shirt on.

"Hey, Maria? Something big happening?" her lover, David, asked. He was still naked as she was moving to get fully clothed in mere seconds.

"Yeah. It's pretty big if I think it is what it is. I'll talk to you as soon as I know something," she said. She looked around for her left boot.

"It's under the chair, Maria. And I'll be back in about three days. I'm heading out to the outer perimeters to get heat and radiation readings," he said.

Maria's swift movements stopped entirely and she looked at him.

"Three days! Damn it!"

Her hands shot to her dark hair, through which she ran her fingers like a comb.

"I'm sorry, honey bee, but I'll be back as soon as I can to finish what I started," he said. At that moment he pulled her deep into an embrace and kissed her as if he were heading off to war. She felt light-headed and suddenly aroused. David's presence and touch had a way of pushing every frightening thing away.

"Damn," she said.

Maria would have held on longer but David's strong hands turned her around and pushed her toward the sliding door and slapped her butt as she moved.

"Three days, love," he said.

Once in the hall on the other side of her residential door, she moved slowly to allow her eyes to adapt to the slightly brighter light in the main corridors. Since it was in the middle of a sleeping cycle for Alpha shift, she was not surprised to see few people in the narrow walkways. As David's image and its wonderful aftereffects faded, she used the ten-minute walk to the Welcome Center to focus on the nuances of the Lazarus protocol.

Hmm. Lazarus…raising someone from the dead. Usually something global and could be catastrophic. Three packages? Three people from the lunar colonies? Pretty damn risky for them to smuggle their way down here.

"So boss? What's the deal?" asked Hector Mendez when he met her in the hall heading to the Welcome Center. "I was having a great dream about it raining when the chief called me."

Maria looked at him and was impressed that he was in full security uniform and not a hair out of place.

"What do you do? Sleep in your uniform?"

"The raining dream got me up to go to the bathroom so I was already on the move and down in the lavatory when the call came in," he said.

"And you always wear your uniform when you are outside your quarters?"

"Why, yes, boss. I'm chief of security. I'm always on," he said. Even as he spoke, his deep voice could not hide some of the sarcasm.

"All right, constable. Remind me to help you with recruitment of officers," she said.

"That would be much appreciated, boss. Nearly all my guys and gals are over forty-five. Smart and seasoned, but I need a whole lot of recruits and young ones to do some of the heavy lifting," he said.

With the exception of four other citizens, seven sleeping dogs, and three cats, they were pretty much the only ones conducting business. As they walked an additional ten minutes toward the receiving room, he gave her a status reports of the day's events, ongoing investigations, and upcoming events that would need additional overtime to make sure the areas were secure. He was just wrapping up his report when they were both in front of the main door from the Welcome Area to the receiving room. She keyed in her code and the heavy door opened smoothly all the way, letting them both into a smaller room attached to the personal transport ramp.

"You know, at some point, you might want to consider putting more barriers between the residential area and the Welcome Center and transport to the surface. It's likely that one of our smart-ass teens will try to take a joyride to the surface," the constable said.

"Noted," Maria replied.

Who the hell would want to go up there? Work, sleep, produce, and stay chained to their technology? I don't know how they do it. My God, they're so boring.

Her thoughts were interrupted by the sudden appearance and deceleration of a personal transport vehicle. In less than a minute, the transport's doors silently opened, and one man and two women emerged. While they were wearing the formal dark suits of the corporate surface dwellers above, their deliberate, economical movements, physiques, and eyes scanning the entire area spoke of something she had not seen for years except in old news reports.

"Now they're the most active military I ever saw. For moon dwellers in less gravity, these three look in pretty good shape," Mendez said. Maria nodded in agreement. She was about to smile and extend her hand to greet them when the lead man responded as if the prior comment had been meant for him to hear.

"We have been in covert operations in the field for the last five years, Security Chief Mendez," the male said. He extended his hand to Maria and shook it as he continued speaking. His grip was like a vise and she was glad when he released her.

"My name is Captain Maximilian Douglas, and my two team members are Lieutenant Roberta Lee and Sergeant Martha Owen. We are part of the Lunar Combined Military Force & Intelligence branch," the man said.

His voice was not as deep as the constable's but it was as firm as his grip.

"Well...nice to meet you. I guess you already know that I'm Maria Henry, plant boss?"

"Yes, ma'am. Nice to meet you," he said.

An unexpected silence fell over the scene. Maria found herself reeling from the flood of information and the invocation of the Lazarus protocol. Still standing in place, she decided to do what she always did when confronted by a series of events and data she was not happy with.

"Okay, captain. What do I call you?" she asked.

The two women behind the man stole a look at each other that spoke volumes. To the captain's credit, he smirked and visibly relaxed.

"You can call me Max. My mother had a thing for long names of German extraction. What can I call you?"

"You can call me 'boss' or 'Maria.' Never call me 'ma'am.' You can call Mendez 'constable,'" she said.

The man nodded. The two women behind him spoke up. They went by their last names—Lee and Owen.

"All right, no bullshit. Lazarus protocol, lunar military in plain view with the surface walkers, and part of intelligence no less giving it an added layer of pre-lunar secession—"

"We like to call it 'independence,'" Max said. Again, his military facade was gone and a more relaxed, amused person was standing before her.

"Well, they were successful, boss," Mendez said.

"Okay, independence, but this looks like the cold war years just before you guys bowed out and left the nest. Are you guys heading to Mars? Is that the plan? Was that satellite you allegedly sent to investigate our passing rogue planet really a cover to build an empire on Mars? Well, happy trails and good luck. Are we done here?" Maria asked. While it was part in jest, there was a tone of real seriousness to her questions.

"You have to admit it, Max. You lunar types are pretty secretive and only show up when shit is about to fall everywhere," Mendez chimed in. Maria liked it when the constable was around; they worked well together after two decades.

The military captain did very little in the way to deny the merits of the questions and did even less to obfuscate the matter at hand.

"Ten years ago, we discovered very unusual readings of the rogue planet heading our way. Its electromagnetic field was stronger than expected and its gravity was well beyond anything we would have imagined. Also, its size is too big to be a planet. It should be a star," he started.

"Is it still going to pass outside our solar system? There's no issue of collisions, is there?" Maria asked. The mere thought of a planetary collision that would damage Earth's crust and destroy the biosphere was too horrible a thought to consider. But Maria had plans in the vault for that, too.

"No, nothing like that at all. It's outside the solar system and well above the plane of Earth and the moon's orbit," he said. The soldier took a moment to organize his thoughts as if he was distracted by something.

"As you know" he continued, "we did send out two deep space probes to see what was going on with these anomalous readings. The first probe is sending back data that show absolutely insane gravitational strength from this thing. From what the science departments tell me, the gravitational strength there should have crushed the planet. It's nearly two and a half times greater than that of Jupiter and by all accounts should not exist in our universe. At the same time, we noticed that there are other time-space disturbances occurring in the wake of this rogue planet."

Maria felt as if her attention span was at full capacity. She was still trying to figure out what Max was saying when Lee jumped in.

"In other words, boss, this planet is linked to our time and space, but its physical science and laws of nature are operating on another plane of existence. It's like the whole planet is alien to our universe. It's something from another universe where the laws of science and physics are completely different from ours," she explained.

Maria was silent. Fortunately Mendez spoke next.

"So this rogue planet is from another universe? Not a really large planet from our universe?"

"In short, yes. It's like a physical sample of an entirely different kind of time, space, gravity, and electromagnetic waves that are floating through our universe. Hence the Lazarus protocol," Max said.

"That protocol is about disaster or a near-disaster event with a short window of time to prepare. How does this rogue planet affect us all if it's passing outside our solar system? It doesn't make sense," Maria said.

Max stepped closer to Maria and spoke in a low voice as if to calm her for what was to come.

"Even from outside of the solar system, this thing is pulling ultraviolet rays from our own sun. The gravitational pull from that planet is pretty powerful. It *could* disrupt Earth's orbit and might move it out of its habitual zone. It might even move all the planets out of their orbits. We just don't know for sure."

"Are…are you serious? *What?*"

Lee finally spoke. What she said was far from joyous.

"We have multiple simulations that suggest that the closer this thing gets, the more it will pull at our sun's corona."

Maria's eyes narrowed in confusion. Owen chimed in to fill in the gap.

"It's remotely possible that this planet's passing might increase solar flares and eject a significant amount of matter from the sun. Maybe enough to reduce both its mass and its radiance. The simulation keeps coming up at least a third of the time more frequently than all other projections."

"In that case, our orbit will move out along with all the other planets if the mass of the sun reduces, and it will get real cold if the sun's brilliance dims. It's a real bad day for us all as a species," Max said.

Maria kept looking into the soldier's eyes. They were a pale blue set and his hair was dark. She looked through them to see if she could see into his soul, to see if he was lying.

Why the hell would he lie about something like this? It's too crazy.

"We have data that we would like to share and get your ideas as to whether we are right or wrong or missed something," Owen said for Max. She produced a handful of computer chips and gave them to Mendez.

"No collisions but our orbit might be compromised," Maria said.

"Right now, we aren't seeing collisions in the future, but it's a moving theory. If it's *just* our orbits being disrupted, then the underground power plants and the lunar colonies become prime real estate for those on the planet's surface," Max said.

"Self-contained biospheres with unlimited energy, nuclear and thermal. Plenty of water and our own functional agriculture and food chain," Maria said.

"We'd be like a spaceship. The surface would freeze within years or months. I guess it would depend on how disrupted the orbits become. That would take a lot of mass loss," Mendez added.

Maria looked at the constable, surprised that the security chief was already speculating the end game based on different conditions. Her surprise must have been obvious.

"Basic physics, boss."

"Yeah, right."

"We're there already, but we have a lot fewer people on the moon than you do down here. There is one thing you people are missing," Max continued.

"What's that?" Maria asked.

"Security," Mendez said instead of Max.

Maria looked at him and wondered how he knew. Even as the constable spoke, it was easy to see that his mind was racing.

"We got three military specialists from the moon, not just your standard intelligence agents. That's all they do all day — think security. And these three have been above ground for years, probably assessing strengths and barriers firsthand. Now they're here and telling us this. I'm guessing they see us as possible allies and if necessary, a possible place to live in case the lunar colonies are compromised," he said.

Maria looked back at Max and the others. Both women nodded in agreement as Max spoke.

"If we are wrong, all the underground power plants will need to be fortified against any corporate takeover or sponsored military strike in the future. Maybe you'll even secede."

"You mean declare our independence," Maria corrected.

The man did smile. Maria's mind was now racing as she immediately assessed her resources and what needed to be done. She had been boss of the place for twenty-two years. It all came to her in the form of puzzle pieces.

Is there time?

"Yes, independence. That's if we're all wrong. But if we're right and Earth's orbit is compromised to an extinction-level event, the underground becomes a massive spaceship for the human species. While we are prepared, if something were to go wrong in our world, we need to have a plan B. As you can see, we have a vested interest in your survival to form this alliance," he finally said.

"And what about our corporate cousins on the surface?" Maria asked.

The empty reception area was quiet yet again for a long moment.

"I would tell them after we have helped you secure all entrances and exits to all nine power plants."

"How long do we have until this FUBAR happens? I want to clear my calendar," the constable asked.

"Five years we think before we feel it all, if anything. It should take us two to three years to prepare here and the others. By then, we will have a small fleet of transports for many of our people if the lunar colonies don't survive," Owen said.

"*Many* of your people?" Maria asked.

"We might have to make some hard decisions we would prefer never to have to make. If we experience a significant failure, thirty percent of our population, women, children, and scientists, will be on the first waves out. The children will be able to adapt to Earth's gravity more easily, we hope. The rest of us will remain," Max said. It was the first time Maria had seen the virile soldier appear sad and small at the same time.

"And we speculate that your capacity might be able to accommodate that number, but we'd have to see," Lee added.

"We're hoping, but we three have been planet-side for years. It took us a long time to get used to Earth's gravity," Owen added.

Maria looked down for a moment. In less than an hour, her entire role had changed from running an oversized power plant for her biosphere to overseeing an ark to preserve the species.

"Shit," she said.

"I second that, boss," Mendez said in agreement.

AD 2142–Wyoming, Two Miles under Earth's Surface

Examine the contents, not the bottle. —The Talmud

"Are you sure we're going to be getting the transmission at the same time your people do?" Maria asked.

"We'll be getting it in less than ten minutes," Max said. He looked at Owen, who nodded to confirm.

The plant control center was busier than usual, and since it was always busy, it was far more chaotic, frenzied, and rushed as staff moved from one console to another, confirming figures and shouting out statuses and numbers. Maria stood in the middle of the large control room holding her own tablet and looking at her own bank of monitors. To her left, the energy and export chief, Mark Dempsey, was on his headset, talking to a number of different engineers and logistics specialists out in the field at the farthest reaches of the plant. To her right was the constable, talking to his own security team and the newly developed military team leader, Lieutenant Julia Rose, a woman who had to be in her late thirties. Once her security chief finished talking to his field officers and the lieutenant went off to her own separate bank of monitors, Maria nodded her head at him to ask him a question.

"Is it me or is she kind of old? I mean, I'm glad Max and his team helped put together our own little army, but I thought they were looking for the young ones. The other three officers are almost as old as she is. What's the deal?"

"We're looking for leadership qualities and experience to deal with volatile situations. She's a teacher," Mendez started.

"A teacher? She has experience in dealing with hostile situations and dangerous people? A teacher?" Maria asked.

"She taught high school for the last fifteen years. She's taught literature and history and had the highest success rate in student attendance and the students had the highest grades. And the guys who think they're hard assess came out from her class smart and reformed. She's a natural leader, boss."

It took Maria mere seconds to understand the connections. It was an understatement to say the miners were rowdy, smart, and opinionated with a healthy dose of raw emotions at the very surface. Add adolescents to the mix and it was as if all those qualities were on steroids.

"Makes sense to me," she said. "Now who's going to teach her youths now?"

"That was a big problem until a guy came in from the surface two years ago. Name is Gabriel Lawless," Mendez started.

"His name is *Lawless*? He had a name like that and lived up on the surface? No wonder they got rid of him."

"Their loss was our major gain. He's great with the kids. Rough around the edges. I'm surprised he didn't get here sooner, but that's me."

Maria nodded as she mulled over the new teacher's name. Mendez turned back to his headset and bank of monitors just as Owen and Lee came up to consult. Maria turned back at her own monitors and looked at the roster of those assigned to the perimeters, especially the two-mile-long rail system. Much to her chagrin, she was closely monitoring the project of setting charges along the tunnels in case all of civilization above them fell into chaos and Central Corporate Command decided to simply take over the underground plants for their own survival.

"Almost done," she said to herself.

She looked closely at the project and saw that the fire teams were behind schedule but moving quickly. David had been clear that there were two ways to collapse a tunnel. One way was to rig it so that when it was blown, digging out would be next to impossible.

"That's easy," he had said. "But we'll never see the surface again and eventually lose air."

Much to her surprise, collapsing key sections and specific parts would be very effective in keeping out intruders for months and allow them to dig out, but it took a lot of time to calculate and implement.

Very long process but good plan.

She looked at the roster and saw that David's name was not on the lead team today.

Thank God!

Maria's mind wandered to how the other power plants were doing with their preparations. Since the lunar team came to them and broke the news, she and Power Plant Six had become the unofficial leaders of the entire underground movement. Her world had also received an unprecedented increase in population from the agricultural and ocean sectors. Upon hearing the news from their underground cousin, the farming and fishing leaders had decided to transition all their youths under twelve years old and women under thirty-two who wanted to leave. Her small city of fifteen thousand miners had now grown to twenty-five thousand.

Surprisingly, the five-year transition had gone smoothly,

especially with the additional skills and resources the new miners brought with them.

I wish we could have worked with the corporate command like the others. Just great.

"Transmission is coming in. If all goes well, we'll have a split screen. One with our lunar command and the other a direct feed to what the probe is seeing," Max explained.

The control room dimmed just a bit as the large floor-to-ceiling screen came to life.

"Lee? Mendez? Make sure you send what we got directly to the Mainframe Control upstairs. Maybe they'll run it," Maria said.

"If it's good news for them, they will," Owen commented.

The left side of the screen showed very serious-looking lunar scientists strapped to their seats so as to keep from floating.

Now why do they need straps if they're sitting still?

Suddenly, there was a burst of cheers and shouts of glee. Their sudden motion explained the wisdom of the safety belts. Others in the back of the view hugged and kissed each other, and as a result were floating in the direction of the greatest force.

The right side captured a star field only.

"Where's the planet?" Dempsey asked.

Maria was wondering the same thing, too, until she realized that near the center of the screen was a sphere of blackness as if there were a black, solid object blocking out the stars behind it. As the camera angle focused on the lower part of the view, the sun's reflection dimly illuminated the leading edge of the planet.

"Is our sun reflecting on the bottom part of the rogue?" Owen asked.

No one answered in the control room, but a series of data, diagrams, and computer-generated images outlined that the massive rogue planet was well above the orbits of all the planets and the sun.

"Well, that's good news," Max said aloud.

The lunar control room which had been loud and noisy five minutes earlier was now deadly silent except for sounds from clicking computers, recycling air, and people exhaling. As Maria and her team listened in on the lunar scientists' communication, the images and animated models were flashing different scenarios based on the new data and their projections. After a minute of flashing, a fresh computer-generated trajectory and filters projected the rogue planet's course and effect.

Maria watched intently. Time passed. How much time? She had no idea.

The image showed the dark planet speeding up as it approached the sun. In addition to its massive size, the rogue planet's speed was unnaturally fast. Its course put it well above and beyond the solar system plane, but its passing was about one point six astronomical units directly above the sun, or a bit farther than Mars's orbit. While that was a relief, as the planet came closer and its illumination grew, the sun's coronal mass ejections increased in both frequency and intensity as the proximity increased. As the sun's filaments grew still longer and became more violent, the ejection of plasma and mass was impressive. Only the computers could assess and compute the mass being ejected. Maria knew there was energy well above and below the range of visible light. More time passed. Her shirt was nearly soaked through with sweat just like everyone else's.

"Holy shit," Dempsey said. "The sun's mass…the sun is blowing out its mass! Look where it's going!"

Maria looked at her monitors and back up to the larger one. On the left side, the scientists' joy and enthusiasm had long vanished and had been replaced with determined brows and ashen expressions.

"Dempsey! Cut to full screen on the right side," Maria said.

The split screen continued and didn't change. She looked back at her energy and export chief and saw that he was frozen like everyone else, staring at the images that were playing out.

"Mark? Enlarge the right side," Maria said again. She watched him shake out of his trance and moved his hands to comply. The serious-looking lunar scientists and personnel vanished and the computer simulation enlarged.

As their own sun dimmed, the rogue planet's illumination was blinding. Then, without warning, the rogue planet flickered and winked out of existence, as if it were never there.

Maria looked at the empty screen and blinked her eyes many times. She looked around the room to see if she was the only one looking for the rogue planet that had illuminated instantaneously to the level of the sun and then just disappeared.

"Did it blow up or something?" someone asked from belowdecks.

"It's like it reached critical mass, or something," Maria said aloud.

"Chief? Roll back the time index to before the rogue starts flickering and focus on the inner planets," Mendez said. Maria was still grappling with the entire scene, but she did notice something in the constable's voice. It was something she'd never heard from him.

Fear? From him?

The angle changed and the images went backward to the

point requested. As it went forward once again, a series of calculations and numbers flickered beside Mercury, Venus, Earth, and Mars. After a brief scan, it was clear that as the mass of the sun decreased significantly. The loss of mass was at a rate not possible based on the numbers. A series of monitors was running and repeating the computations and projections. The silence of the room was deafening. More time passed. More silence interrupted only by clicking, breathing, and air circulating.

"Talk to me, people," Maria said eventually.

"Rebooting mainframe and backup for confirmation on data," a female voice said.

"Pulling up most likely simulation on the main screen," the chief added.

"Lunar command is running its own series of numbers and it's looking grim. Owen—check my numbers," Max said.

"I keep coming up with the same data and simulations: the sun's gravity has weakened. This is allowing the orbits of the planets to expand outward," Lee said aloud.

There was more silence, as if Lee had pronounced their death sentence.

We are so screwed...

"Speed up the simulation of the planets' orbits and put them on the main screen, full size," Maria instructed.

She already knew the answer. As the time indexes sped up while months passed rapidly into years, the chief stopped the time at the seven-year mark, AD 2149. By then, the orbits of all the planets were profoundly different and the entire solar system was changed. The Earth was still outside the asteroid belt but was beyond Mars's original orbit. Mars was ablaze with impact craters and volcanic activity as stray comets and asteroids were caught in its gravity well from entering the retreating asteroid field, while Neptune and Uranus were no longer held in orbit at all. As the orbits shifted, the sun's ejections of plasma had continued to accelerate, showing no sign of slowing.

"Earth's orbit at this point is about seven hundred twenty-four point ninety-five days," another voice from belowdecks said.

"We're going to need a whole new set of calendars," Mendez commented.

"The sun is still losing a massive amount of mass," Max said.

"It's like that rogue planet started a chain reaction or something," Owen commented.

"That thing accelerated our sun's life to a red dwarf," the chief said. His tone was that of resignation.

"And disappeared. How the hell does that happen? A planet that size?" Lee asked. Hearing her voice again reminded Maria that the plan to move their defensive perimeters was no longer critical.

The time index sped up to AD 2200. The chief stopped it there because the computer-generated simulation looked very different. He dialed it back to replay several more times before Maria spoke.

The planets Earth, Venus, and Mercury joined the rest of the solar system as they reached their orbital escape velocity and were hurtling into deep space. The sun had dimmed to a much smaller, pale red sphere. The newly formed red dwarf star that replaced the powerful, younger solar system sun had no mass to hold the planets in place.

"This scenario should happen over billions of years and it will all happen in decades. What the hell…" the chief added.

"All right. The very thing we feared would happen,

happened. That means we accelerate all defensive perimeters and secure all life support. We do this right, we live underground and the lunar colony goes on as usual," Maria said. As much as she wanted to crawl into a corner with David and sleep, she needed to keep her team going, focused and positive.

"People…we knew this would happen," she said again.

"Except about the disappearing rogue planet," Max said.

While Maria wasn't a scientist, her position of power plant boss meant she knew a lot about physics, numbers, and the role of mass and gravity. She decided to appeal to everyone's desire to figure things out to shake them out of their trance.

"How the hell does a rogue planet alter our sun's progression so that it goes from our sun to a red dwarf in hours?" she asked.

"It may have been depleting our sun for years prior at a different wavelength," Owen offered.

"And the sun continued ejecting mass after the planet disappeared," Lee added.

No other answers came for a long minute until Max spoke again. Maria started thinking of another strategy.

"I guess, boss, the scientists were right. That thing is not just a rogue planet. It's from another universe or plane of existence. I guess shit like that can happen when you're talking alternative universes and altered existence with other laws of physics."

With more than forty people in the control room, it was still quiet. The notion of the silent people triggered a thought.

"Mendez? Did all of this play up on the surface? Do the regular people know?" she asked.

Her chief of security needed to look over his monitors to figure it out.

"They cut it off before all the data were obtained. Looks like central corporate control is keeping its citizens in the dark," Mendez said.

"Shit. You know what that means, people?" Maria said.

"Our home just became prize real estate like all the other power plants underground," Mendez said.

"All of a sudden, the lunar colonies' self-contained and safe world looks pretty good," Max added.

"We got to move, people," Maria said to forty people. In mere seconds, the activity went from zero to ninety. Orders, data, and confirming information filled the air with a profound sense of urgency as people mobilized to keep their home safe.

Maria nodded in approval. She was glad that her people could get beyond the horrors of the future and focus on preserving themselves. She felt a rush of anxiety, however, but it was not about the Earth or even herself.

Where are you, David?

AD 2142 (Four Days Post-Event)– Wyoming, Two Miles under Earth's Surface

Sorrow for those who disappear never to be found. —The Talmud

"Not now," Maria whispered. Her residential door's chimes had been ringing every fifteen minutes for the last hour. While she had secluded herself in her quarters for only three hours, she saw everything that was happening to her power plant via her monitors and tablets. When needed, she even jumped in to answer questions and provide leadership. Presently, she was still in bed, fully dressed and surrounded by a series of tablets as if she were in a nest. While the warning lights flashed yellow silently, indicating that the station was to remain at a hypervigilant status, the actual threat had passed days ago. The rogue planet had passed well above the solar system, depleted their sun of mass and plasma, converting it from a strong yellow sun to a weak red dwarf star, and then the rogue planet vanished through some kind of wormhole. Immediately after, the Earth along with all the other planets rapidly expanded orbit away from the sun due to the sun's loss of mass. At least that was how she understood it. And while that was on a grand scale of events, it was the mundane that crushed her. She sifted through her tablets and found the roster of the nine dead miners who'd set off the tunnel mines to keep Central Corporate Command's military from using them to gain entrance and seize her power plant, to take her world for their elite and military.

They had no problem with the idea of letting us and everyone else die.

"Why, David," she said quietly. "You knew I wouldn't do it, didn't you? You knew I wouldn't push the button if you and the others were still out there."

Her eyes were depleted of tears as she had cried them all in the first two days while still at her post. Her mind drifted to the minutes that followed her lover's death, when she realized he'd made the decision to save her and his home instead of letting her do it. And after that, Central Corporate Command had well articulated its threats and demands that she and all other power plant bosses were to be relieved of their posts and to expect "replacement personnel in three hours." When she and the other bosses went radio silent, the orders to walk away shifted to "comply or suffer catastrophic consequences."

They've already taken my love, my life away, she had thought.

Finally, when Command threatened to use biological weapons of mass destruction on her underground world, she made a decision to shorten Earth's life on the surface from years to months; she cut off all power to them. Military, offices, hospitals, anything in need of electricity was turned off in the entire eastern part of the continent known as North America. When the other power plants saw what she'd done, they followed suit without hesitation. Tunnels collapsed, power to surface dwellers was shut down, and her love forever gone, she now lay down in her bed alone. She mulled over everything that had happened and realized that David was right. If he hadn't done what he did, she might not have made the decisions that followed. In her state of mind as it was now, she would kill the world for losing David. Well, she had, at least those on the surface.

Her door chimed again.

"Go away," she said.

Instead, her locked residence door opened as if it were unlocked with an override code. She knew who it was even before his dark image appeared at her bedroom doorway. Chief Constable Mendez did not apologize for the intrusion or explain why he was there. He just stood quietly and waited for her to talk. In another state of mind, she was sure she would have thrown a fit, but she was not herself. Minutes passed until she spoke.

"I hate them all, constable. If it wasn't for them, David would be alive. If they weren't such emotionless automatons, we could have saved their children. But they wanted everything. They wanted our world so their elite heartless bastards could live here at the expense of us and everyone else," she said. Her tone and presentation were void of all emotions except sadness.

Mendez nodded. For a security chief, he was a good reader of character and listened well. He let the silence sit for a moment. She watched the large man shifting from one foot to the next, looking down at his feet as he often did when he was listening intently.

"I can't tell you it's going to get better or if you'll ever heal, boss. Only time and God can do that," he said quietly.

"Yeah," she muttered.

"But I can say this," he added quickly.

Maria could still feel her heart pick up at the thought of

getting an answer for something she could not fathom to ever understand.

"Boss? What would David want you to do right now?" Mendez asked.

Maria found herself looking at her security chief. She wanted to leap across the room and strike him. Her heart raced and her breath came up short. But after just a second, she actually heard what the constable had said.

What would David want me to do?

She sighed and felt her heart settle back down. She released her balled fists and relaxed her entire body. After a minute more, she moved her array of tablets from the bed so she could get up. As soon as her feet touched the ground, she stood and looked right at him.

"He'd be pissed that I was not doing my job and would say something stupid, like most men would," she said.

Mendez nodded and looked back down at his feet again.

"We're pretty good at saying stupid things, boss."

She was just pulling up a couple of choice words and colorful metaphors for how the constable had manipulated her emotions to get her going, when her quarter's intercom came alive.

"Sorry to bother you, boss, but is the constable there?" Lieutenant Julia Rose asked.

Maria could see that her friend's shoulders physically slumped before he spoke.

"Here, lieutenant," he said.

"Just so you know, our 'Teacher of the Year' just left the tavern three sheets to the wind, and was heard saying he planned to get to the surface 'no matter what.' I'm heading Welcome Center Three and there's already a group of security en route. Problem is, they don't have any stun guns," she said.

"The guy's in his forties, right? My team stationed there is trained and far younger," Mendez explained.

"Ah, all right. But I wouldn't count on him going down easy. He's a father bear searching for his cubs and won't go gentle into that good night," the lieutenant said.

Maria wondered about her choice of words. Her puzzled expression caught Mendez's attention.

"All right, lieutenant. I'll meet you at the center and maybe you can talk him down. And don't use any of that literature stuff. It confuses us all," he said.

"No promises. See you in ten," she said.

Maria looked at him and could see he was not happy.

"It's Lawless, isn't it?" she said.

"Sure is," he answered.

Maria had met the newcomer once and liked him immediately. For a former surface dweller, he had a lot of attitude and spunk. He was also courageous. There would have been thirty dead if it weren't for him and some of the older students who'd pulled some of the miners from the rubble from the collapsed tunnels.

The constable remained in place. She nodded and stood up on her aching feet.

"All right, constable. I got your point and will rip you a new one later," she said.

"No problem, boss. You heading to the control room?"

"Yup. That's what David would have wanted me to do," she said.

Without a further word, she walked out of her bedroom and quarters into a very crowded common hallway with Mendez right behind her.

"You deal with Lawless and I'll check in with the chief and Delta shift. Let me know what happens," she said.

71

The constable turned left as she continued straight to the control center.

"Will do, boss."

She walked in silence, though her once relatively empty common ways were filled with multiple personnel, dogs, and cats.

"I know, David. I'm going to work," she said quietly to herself.

Hell—Part Four

Rogue Planet—Infinity—Alien Biosphere

The sun will set without thy assistance. —The Talmud

"Cartographer, rise," the voices ordered.
Consciousness emerged for the first time in millennia.
"Am I the last to awake?"
"Yes. All the others have been engaged."
"Have we arrived?" the Cartographer asked.
"Yes, Cartographer. What will the heading be?"
The Cartographer shifted its consciousness toward the igneous crust of their planet facing the strong yellow star. The warm rays of the alien young sun of the small solar system were perfect. Passing right over it, the Cartographer assessed that the energy levels in the quartz strata were rising after billions of years of depletion, the time when they entered this strange, alien universe. While the sun's energy had been feeding their home for years prior at multiple wavelengths, the proximity would be just what was needed for terminal velocity. The carbon deposits awaited the planet's mantle spin to reach launch velocity, and the iron's electromagnetic field was near full capacity. All the other minerals, rocks and strata were primed to escape this infernal place.
"I will not miss this universe," the voices said.

"Why?"

The Cartographer knew why but wanted to hear other voices. He appreciated the rest and the escape from the alien universe's void, but there was time before propulsion reached critical mass to bend time and space, and the absence of the voices was missed.

"I will not miss its silence."

"Yes. Surrounded by those of our own kind—silicate, mica, quartz, feldspar, iron, diamond—all around us and yet they remain trapped to themselves, silent, devoid of sapience. How is this possible? This is a place of no hope," the Cartographer answered.

"Nitrogen, oxygen, hydrogen, carbon-based life and light waves that act as both particle and waves are all very disturbing," the voices added.

"Still, we will only be able to reach the halfway mark if all goes well. It will always be to the halfway mark. Forever."

"Yes. But maybe there will be others. Maybe more of our kind. Something to end the loneliness," the voices countered.

"Yes. At least that."

The Cartographer was nearly done with the required measurements and location to open a portal to finally escape this hell. The igneous crust was reaching a critical level and the diamond engines were near launch. The yellow sun's mass and energy were perfect. The planet's molten core sped up the iron mantle's photon buildup and the electromagnetic field expanded exponentially to provide shielding for transport.

"Are you sure there is no life of our kind on these other terrestrial planets?" the Cartographer asked.

"No. They are all like the others in this place. Silence. Water. Elements. Carbon. No life as we understand it. Void. Emptiness. We long to escape this hell," the voices said in unison and pathos.

The Cartographer felt through the crust near the quartz beds and the igneous surface that all mass and energy extracted from the yellow sun were now at a perfect level. The mantle was at nominal levels, propulsion was initiated and the shielding was fully charged from the iron core. The internal mantle rotated faster, allowing the electromagnetic field to multiply in strength. More carbon beds were pressurized to form diamonds in case of engine failure. The emitting energy would increase their velocity to leave the barren universe.

"We are ready, Cartographer."

"Yes. I will not miss this place. Do you think the next universe will at least have sapience of our kind?"

"We will see."

"Yes."

The heat and vibrations of the planet's surface erupted outward and focused on one specific spot of space just ahead of its position. The fabric of time and space thinned at first and then expanded in brilliant light. After mere seconds, the barrier between universes opened and a conduit to another universe with its own natural laws, intelligence, and life awaited their arrival. As the rogue planet flashed and launched deeper into the corridor between universes, the voices spoke again.

"I hear voices on the other side, Cartographer. Similar to our own…"

After taking billions of years to travel, the Cartographer held the course and waited.

"Finally."

Limbo–Part Five

Earth—AD 2145—Ruins of Merrimack College, Twenty-five Miles from Boston, Massachusetts

Make your books your companions. —The Talmud

"Marsha? Marvin? What are you doing out here? It is very cold," Rebekah Lawless said.

Marvin turned to see his mother struggling to get up the small rise to meet them on the empty, ancient road. While devoid of obstacles such as wheeled, tractor, and rail vehicles, it was the recently fallen snow over the permafrost and the protective multilayers of clothes she wore that were making it difficult for her to get traction and leverage. He moved toward her and pulled her up, since his footing was better placed in frozen footprints from that same morning. As he pulled her up, he looked behind her to make sure that the hatch to their old clubhouse was closed. She was right, however. Even in his multiple layers and covered face, it was remarkably cold. The sun's rays were diffused by the near constant cloud cover, giving it a more pinkish hue instead of its new red color. It was about one-third the size it had been just a few years ago.

"June 21, 2145, and the sun is as bright as a street lamp in dense fog," he heard Marsha say.

Marvin felt the corners of his mouth curl up at her use of images rather than her old efficient vernacular.

She's been reading stories again.

"Why would you use those images when simply stating that the sun's illumination is a third the strength and the fog is obscuring its limited radiance and warmth?" he heard his mother say.

Poor thing. She can't give it up.

With his mother and sister beside him, Marvin returned to looking at Boston's dark, frozen skyline in the early afternoon on the summer solstice. The once thriving metropolis was motionless and empty. None of the telltale signs of life was visible, no aircraft, rail traffic, or movement of any kind. With the lowest tier of the food chain knocked out, all vegetation, insects, animals, and humans were either dead or dying on the frozen planet. Surrounded by frozen, bare trees, his small family unit was the only visible life overlooking the empty vast plain toward the city. It was strange to see nothing in the sky. No drones. No aircraft. No sounds or light.

In the silence of early afternoon, Marvin imagined that in the old days when Earth was closer to its sun, the silence and stillness of the city might have been something experienced in the early morning at the break of dawn. Even then, there would be drones, rail traffic and aircraft. He remembered standing near the same place with his father and Marsha more than a decade earlier. There was nothing but life—the movement above and around Boston could be easily seen once the overgrown fields were cleared of vegetation, small animals, and so many bugs and birds.

It was so warm then.Look at this place, he thought. The vista always made him sad.

"So with a total of fifteen hours of sunlight scheduled for

today, it's pretty close to freezing, I bet," Marsha said parenthetically. At every intake and exhale of precious air, the freezing vapors punctuated the fact that the atmosphere was very cold. And while breathing in the frigid air did not sting as much during the day, it was in the outside, nighttime air that breathing hurt more than exposure to the cold air that was well below zero.

"Yup. Not exactly the dog days of summer," Marvin added.

The family continued looking at the dark city's outlines until another cloud bank began to move in from the east. It was easy to see that dark, heavy clouds were also moving toward their barren, silent real estate. Marvin heard his mother speak in a rare moment of reflection. Her voice in the past several months had been weaker than usual, as if she were tired.

"It would have been logical to stay in the sanctioned safe zones in Maine," she said.

A flash of anger came over Marvin. He focused on watching his emotions so he could talk to his mother in a tone that she would understand. Strong emotions didn't work with most people. *That is when there were people.*

Marvin collected his thoughts before he spoke in an even tone that was forced.

"So that our *stepfather* could monitor our deaths from the comfort of his safe haven? Where he could be sure that we perished? I wouldn't give him the satisfaction." Marvin took a deep breath of the frigid air. It was very difficult to contain raw emotions now. With most of the people gone, it didn't matter so much. *Nine billion to maybe twelve million and dropping. God...*

"Screw him!" Marsha added.

"He might have been able to suggest that another, less

efficient and less valuable personnel be sent out and we take their place," Rebekah said weakly.

"He had that chance for two months, Mother! And he did nothing. He wasn't going to do anything for us," Marsha said.

Her harsh tone took Marvin by surprise. But Marvin nodded in approval. Marsha had long resisted Marvin's plan to escape to the old ruins where his father and they used to explore. It was fun back when they were nine and seven. But when it became clear that their time on the Earth's surface was limited and that only the "multifaceted, efficient and gifted" would be taken into Central Corporate Command's arks, Marvin watched his sister's steadfast loyalty to her stepfather wane and collapse when he alone was chosen to leave. In less than thirty minutes, his stepfather had packed some belongings and left his family behind.

He didn't even take any pictures.

If Marvin's mother hadn't insisted on following his stepfather's trail and waiting for him to rethink and take them in, they would have had three additional months to stockpile their own ark. While Marvin had started years prior, he still lost valuable time.

That's time we'll never get back.

"He cost us," he said bitterly. He couldn't keep the emotion out of his voice at the lost time.

Marvin was sure his mother was going to offer some response but was interrupted by a very young voice.

"Hey! Come on back in here! It's freezing," a seven-year-old voice yelled out. Marvin pushed away his angry thoughts about his stepfather's abandonment and focused on important things. He turned to see a little boy waving to him to come back in. The young boy was one of five children, ranging from seven to thirteen, whom they'd picked up along the way.

While billions were dead and more dying every day and in the bitter cold night, there were orphans who chose to search for help rather than to passively wait for death.

Marvin waved back and turned to help his mother and sister down the small embankment. By the time they were halfway to the ancient basement metal door in the old abandoned Engineering wing of a university, a sudden squall of snow burst above them. He was thankful Jim had called them back. While they had only a short distance to travel, the snowstorm's sudden blinding appearance was commonplace on their cold planet. When it wasn't snowing small, dry crystals or when there was a break in the heavy, frozen clouds, the stars were so close and it made them feel as if they were the last people in a dark and empty world.

Maybe we are now. At least on the surface, he thought. The irony was not lost on him how those relegated to the power plant cities underground or the independent moon colony were safe, warm, and probably prepared, while the reasonable, efficient, and productive citizens on the surface were all dead or doomed.

Stop it, Marvin! That negativity doesn't help!

"It's crazy how fast the storms hit now," Marsha shouted out over the howling wind.

"And the snow doesn't even make good snowballs," Marvin said in an attempt at humor.

"Not sticky enough," Marsha said.

"Well, that is because the lack of moisture at lower levels and colder air patterns at the surface keep the liquid to a minimum. With no surplus of moisture in the air, the snow cannot collect to form a snowball," their mother said.

Marvin closed his eyes and kept his mouth shut.

"That was humor, Mother," Marsha finally said.

After a very short trek and carefully navigating the stairs six feet belowground, Marvin closed the first of four heavy metal doors leading to the old fallout shelter that had been converted into engineering labs. Their footsteps echoed in the recesses of the old, dark, and deep ruins as their two flashlight beams cut through the darkness. Three doors and three barricading systems later, four more feet farther below the surface, they were at the final door that was held open by an eleven-year-old girl, Debby, who was smiling. She had an open can of multicolored food in syrup called "Fruit Cup." Marvin was happy to see her immediately offer some to Jim, who accepted with zeal.

"Best meal I've had in a week," the cute redhead girl said.

"Wow! Hey, I've saved mine from yesterday. Maybe it's the same kind," Jim said enthusiastically.

Both preteens ran off into a large main room. In the low light, Marvin took off his layers and shook off the snow that held on in the balmy fifty-six-degree work area. Marvin helped his mother take off her layers and then took their clothes to where they kept the other clothing gear and sleeping blankets.

"It is a shame," Rebekah said.

In a moment of hope and curiosity, Marvin waited for her to continue. Marsha was less patient.

"What do you mean now, Mother?"

While it was easy to hear the enmity in his sister's voice toward their mother, he was sure that she'd missed the entire emotional message.

"With our finite resources and eight people, our time alive is shortened," Rebekah said.

Though it was relatively quiet inside the large complex of rooms, the sounds of laughter, giggling, and talking were easily discernible. When compared to the tomb outside their constructed cave, their home was bustling with life and hope. Marvin readily sensed the coming emotional onslaught from his sister.

"So we should have left those kids to die out there? We should have done the logical and reasonable thing your husband did? You know, extend our resources and our lives together at the expense of five children? Is that what you're saying?"

"Marsha…let it go. She doesn't get it," Marvin said in a low tone. He motioned his hands downward and then pointed at the playing children.

Even in the dim room, he could see his sister's anger and his mother's expressionless reaction.

"I hate this," Marsha said. She stormed off toward the youth ostensibly to put distance between herself and her mother.

"I do not understand your sister," Rebekah started to say before Marvin cut her off with the raising of his hand.

He sighed and focused on controlling his anger so he could convey his message without emotions, in the hope that his mother would understand and comply. While only nineteen years old, he felt much older.

"I stopped Marsha's tirade so she would not upset the children and their play. It was not to support your thinking. Do not say those things about resources, time, and what we should or should not have done. It's passed. There's nothing to be done about it, and reiterating the obvious is not helpful and will only provoke anger and frighten the children. Is that reasonable?"

He waited for his mother to respond. It came surprisingly quick.

"Yes," she said. Nothing else followed.

Finally.

Marvin looked around the dark room with its four battery-operated lamps shining in the dark. He moved away from his mother's side, took out his flashlight, and moved to another smaller room. He opened its door, stood at the entrance, and looked at just a few boxes, a mere fraction of what was stored three years ago. What had been a mountain of boxes filled with an assortment of canned water and food, old freeze-dried survival rations, and military field rations was down to just a few large boxes. Everything that was there had been gathered over the course of the five years either online or by physical purchase. All done before the flood of orders took everything. Next he had scoured the old buildings outside Boston before the road vehicles and rails were seized. While weapons were not accessible, blankets, cots, clothes, and other necessities had been carefully collected and put in hiding long before the crisis was evident.

"Forewarned is forearmed. That's something you used to say, Dad," Marvin said to himself.

Marvin's trust of the government had crashed when it was clear that something about the passing rogue planet's sudden drop from the planet-wide media was not right. An old story came to mind. It was a story his father had read to him about a government that hid things from its citizens. And that had got him wondering.

What if the passing planet was bad? What if I have to keep my sister and mother safe? Where would I take them? Where would we go? Where would we all be safe?

The answer came immediately. *The clubhouse.*

With a safe location identified, all he needed to do was stockpile supplies. And while initially he thought he had gone overboard, he had found more books in the old place that spoke of preparing for "end of days" and "what to do when civilization ends" and "how to prepare for the zombie apocalypse." In fact, of all the things he'd bought, found, and recovered, he found a treasure trove of books—novels and stories his father would read to them—to be the most priceless.

"Still, with so few boxes and supplies, we will need to ration more. Eight of us…" he said.

"What are you saying?" he heard Marsha ask from behind him.

"Nothing. I'm just thinking that we'll need to seriously start thinking about doing another inventory of food and water again, and rationing to make sure things last longer," he said.

"Oh," Marsha said.

Instead of starting the task, Marvin closed the door and moved back into the larger room. Even though it was the middle of the day and the cold night was hours away, he decided to take his mind and everyone else's mind off of day-to-day survival with something fun. Following silently behind him, he heard Marsha speak quietly so as not to be heard.

"You're going to read us a story, aren't you?"

"How did you know?" he asked.

"You didn't start the inventory and instead picked up your pace to get in here. I think it's a great idea," she said.

"It's what Dad would do," Marvin said.

Leaning over a makeshift table, he pulled out a large box of discolored old paperback novels. Without looking, Marvin picked a book off the top and read the title and author to his sister for feedback.

"What about this one? *A Pail of Air*, by Fritz Leiber?"

"No," his sister said immediately. She leaned into him and spoke so only he could hear.

"It's too close to our own situation."

"Does it end happily?"

Marvin watched his sister think for a moment and then she answered with a smile.

"Well, actually, it kind of does. There are hardships, but they make it through and are rescued. Pretty hopeful," she explained.

"Sounds to me like a good story before dinner," Marvin said.

Without further discussion, Marvin called all the children together. He had them move two of the large cots close to him and wrap themselves up together in heavy wool blankets. In spite of the disapproving look of his mother, he was glad to hear his sister chastise her quietly.

Someday she might understand.

"Do you have a better suggestion? Something that can spark imagination and pass time?" he heard his sister ask his mother over the din of moving children, cots, and blankets.

Not hearing a response, Marvin pulled an image of how his father would read aloud with great affect, and then act out some parts. As he moved the dim light from one of the only lit candles in use, the flickering light and sound of muffled wind outside provided a perfect atmosphere.

This is just perfect, he thought.

Heaven—Part Six

Moon—AD 2145—Forward Observation Post Nine, Lunar Colony, Northern Rim, Peary Crater

Doubt cannot override a certainty. —The Talmud

"So you think it's a good idea to send the kids to Earth? How come?" Technician Michael Davis asked.

"They'll have a better chance of surviving the planet's gravity, and they'll continue our present on Earth," Technician Azrael Crow said.

Strapped into their comfortable, form-fitting chairs surrounded by hundreds of clinking lights, readouts, and monitors, they had the relatively lonely task of surveying the Earth's new geology and scanning for life via satellite from their self-contained lunar bubble.

"I don't know, Azrael. The colonel's not going to order parents to give up their kids, and I'm not seeing parents just giving up their babies when they could live here with them. Would you?" Michael asked.

"Oh, hell no," Azrael said.

Michael looked at her and smiled. He knew the answer long before he asked.

"Now why the hell do you do that?"

"Do what?"

"Say these things and then say you wouldn't do it, and then go on without even a discussion?"

"Because I know you'll never give up the discussion."

"So you give me the answer that will shut me up? You hate talking, or do you hate talking to just me?" Michael asked.

"That has nothing to do with it. I think we should order parents to do it for the species. But the colonel won't, so no parent would give up their child. And I know I wouldn't either. I'm just saying," Azrael explained.

Michael remained silent for a minute, partly to think of an answer and partly to look at an unusual reading just outside of the Boston metropolis.

Hmm. What is that?

"So you would take a page from Central Corporate Command & Mainframe Control's playbook and break up family units for the purpose of the corporation, planet, and human species? You're pretty messed up, Azrael," Michael continued as he narrowed his field of vision from the satellite orbiting Earth.

"That would be the best way to ensure our survival. Two places to live versus just one. We get hit with one of those stray asteroids that nuked Phobos and Deimos, we'll wish we did," Azrael said in all seriousness.

"Didn't help Earth out. You sure you're not an Earth spy? You know we seceded from Earth," Michael said.

Michael heard some kind of response but his attention was now fully seized by the odd readings. Something he had not seen in at least a year.

Heat signatures? Really?

Michael watched his readings fluctuate. He moved a few levers and keyed in more commands to narrow an orbiting satellite to pinpoint what appeared to be heat signatures on the frozen outskirts of the once thriving city. Anxiety and excitement welled up in his gut. He had seen similar readings before, but then there was only one. With nearly no animal life on Earth bigger than rodents, these three heat signatures were very promising.

"You got something?" Azrael asked. It was easy to tell that she was excited, too. With the primary task of surveying the planet's freezing surface and helping the underground power plants locate planetary hot spots near water sources, it was exceedingly rare for their efforts to morph into a possible rescue operation.

"Hey, what are those coordinates the lieutenant gave us?" Michael asked.

"You mean Douglas from Power Plant Six? That was like three years ago, Michael."

"I know that, Azrael. It's just outside Boston, right?"

"Yup. It's ah…longitude is 42.6677 degrees north and latitude is 71.1225 degrees west."

Michael heard Azrael keying in more commands on her console, and then a slightly larger monitor displayed two ghostlike pinpoints that were initially motionless until one moved and met another that was moving toward the first two.

"Weather patterns cut us a break. You got slight clearing but it looks like a high-pressure system is coming in fast. It's got snow, of course," Azrael said.

"How could they survive all these years?" Michael said to himself.

"That's three years, old calendar, right?" Azrael asked.

Michael didn't answer. He focused on simultaneously uploading the data to the lunar control room and to Power Plant Six. More clicking and movement occurred beside him as he sensed Azrael's levels of excitation increasing by the second.

"They have to be holed up underground," Azrael said.

"I'm expanding the radius to fifty feet to see if there's more," Michael said. He kept his eyes locked on his smaller monitor to make sure he did not lose the heat signatures as they got smaller and the area around them, still dark, was expanded.

"Hey, Michael! I got the exact location—it's them! Holy shit! Those coordinates are gold! How did the lieutenant know? How long has it been?" Azrael asked, her excitement far from containable.

"It's been years, Azrael. Damn. It's been years."

Michael's disposition was deadly serious. He feared that all of a sudden he would lose their signatures and not have an exact location to send help. And help was over twenty-one hundred miles due west and two miles underground. Underground rail would have taken twelve hours when the Earth was efficient and working.

Now? A week maybe to get there.

Michael watched intently as the three figures walked single file northwest of their exact location. As data flashed up on their monitors, the ghostlike silhouettes were fading from view as the snowstorm engulfed them. Panic at losing the figures' heat signatures was about to set in when Michael saw signals just ahead of the trio of a larger area of geothermal heat indicating they were heading to someplace warm.

"You getting this?" Michael asked.

"I got it. Looks like our survivors are heading to an underground shelter. This is crazy, Michael!"

"This is great crazy," he said.

Not taking his eyes off his monitor at all, he watched each signature slowly disappear into the larger heat signal. Once they all were swallowed up, the larger signal vanished as if a door had been closed.

Michael inhaled a deep breath. He realized that he must have been holding his breath all that time.

"I got it all. Time index, location, and possible land route," Azrael said.

Michael forced himself to relax and normalized his breathing. He felt a wave of relief and his nose stuffed up a little. He already felt moisture in the corner of his eyes.

"Are you crying again?" Azrael asked. Her mocking tone was expected.

"Shut up, Azrael. No one likes you," he shot back.

"Crybaby," she said.

Michael chuckled and expanded his search pattern. He planned to switch over to surveying again after he spent another hour looking for other heat signatures while the satellite was close to the signals. He was just catching up on his air when he heard Azrael giving her status report and sending data.

"Control? This is Forward Observation Post Nine *Angel*. Do you copy?"

"Control hears all, *Angel*. What's happening with the survey? I didn't expect to hear from you for another two hours…looks like you uploaded something to us," the voice said over the small command module's control room speaker.

"You're going to love this. We got three heat signatures and a possible shelter below-ground at coordinates 42.6677 degrees north, 71.1225 degrees west. You'll be receiving the log, visuals, and transcript in seconds. Do you copy?" Azrael said. Her excitement was palpable but she kept on task. The response from control was immediate.

"Ah, *Angel*? Are you shitting me? Did you and Michael snag some black market alcohol or something? Where can I get some?" the disembodied voice asked.

Both technicians laughed. It was a good day.

Azrael took a moment to compose herself and then reviewed the mission. Michael drifted off in his thoughts.

Maybe there's others.

About the Author

In addition to the *Birds of Flight* series and other award-winning science fiction stories, Erickson holds a BA in psychology and sociology from Boston College and a master's degree in psychiatric social work from the Simmons School of Social Work. He is senior instructor of psychology and counseling at Cambridge College and a senior therapist in a clinical group practice in the Merrimack Valley, Massachusetts.

Author's Note

If you enjoyed this novel, please feel free to let others know about it. I would also appreciate it if you could leave a review on Amazon, Barnes & Noble, or wherever you purchased the novella. For more information on my other stories, please feel free to visit my websites.

www.jmericksonindiewriter.com

www.jmericksonindiewriter.net